The Jumping-Off Place

The Jumping-Off Place

Dolores White Kiser

iUniverse, Inc.
New York   Bloomington

The Jumping-Off Place

iUniverse books may be ordered through booksellers or by contacting:

iUniverse
1663 Liberty Drive
Bloomington, IN 47403
www.iuniverse.com
1-800-Authors (1-800-288-4677)

Because of the dynamic nature of the Internet, any Web addresses or links
contained in this book may have changed since publication and may no longer be
valid. The views expressed in this work are solely those of the author and do not
necessarily reflect the views of the publisher, and the publisher hereby disclaims
any responsibility for them.

ISBN: 978-1-4401-9818-2 (sc)
ISBN: 978-1-4401-9819-9 (ebk)

Printed in the United States of America

iUniverse rev. date: 02/12/2010

Chapter One

Sixteen-year-old Maria Grant's heart pounded like a drum beating at a Choctaw powwow. Looking down, she watched the flounce at the top of her red dress bounce each time her heart thumped. Why had she let Austin talk her into riding to Granny's with a man she didn't even know? Yeah, it saved money rather than buying a bus ticket, but who was this stranger?

Always searching, her conscience nagged. She glanced at Austin Lincoln, the boy she'd known most of her life, sitting in the backseat beside her. He finished cracking the knuckles on his right hand and then started on the left hand.

Just like me . . . as nervous as a cat in a room full of rockers, she decided.

Maria nudged Austin. "Are you scared?" she whispered.

Eli, the mysterious driver, glanced over his shoulder at the two students. "Huh?"

"Nothing. Maria was talking to me," Austin answered. Maria watched him swallow a big lump in his throat. He turned to frown at her.

"Be quiet," Austin whispered.

Maria's nervousness turned into downright fear when Eli turned the car onto an unfamiliar one-lane road. *Is this the road to Granny's? Why is Eli driving on this pig trail? Should've gone to the conference with Mama and Papa.* She wanted to tell Austin about her fears, but she knew Eli would gripe at her again.

Maria felt her shoulders sagging. Could Eli be trusted? She turned to look out the window to hide the tears welling up. She didn't want Austin to know she was about to cry. Through blurry eyes, she gazed at the tall pines.

Why can't we just go to Granny's house without wandering around all over creation?

An Indian man came into view, staggering up the road. He wore a wide-brimmed black hat that looked as if dust had been sifted around the edge and it had settled into the folds. A band of colorful beadwork encircled the crown. The man held a small dog to his chest. As he walked along, he stumbled and nearly fell. Maria poked Austin in the ribs. He jumped.

"Look at the man carrying that little black dog," she said, aloud.

"What?" Eli asked. He took his eyes off the sandy ruts for a moment and the car careened into deep sand.

"I wanted Austin to look at that cute black dog," Maria said, pointing toward the animal.

"Don't talk so loud when I'm driving in this sand," grumbled Eli. He raced the motor, but the car wouldn't move. The veins in the side of his neck seemed about to ready to pop when he tightened his grip on the steering wheel. Trying to drive out of the sand was like a child pulling his foot out of a house made of sand without collapsing the walls. His attempts never worked. Expelling a deep breath, Eli opened the car door and stepped out. He stood gazing at the deep sand. "I wonder how we'll get this car out of here." Turning to Maria he grouched, "Why did you bother me anyway, Miss know-it-all?"

Maria wanted to shrink into a ball the size of the dog and hide, but she knew that was impossible.

"Maybe that man can help find a team of horses to pull us out," Austin suggested.

"A team of Choctaws would do, but we don't have one. You'll have to get out and help push this buggy through the sand."

"But, we're on our way to my granny's house," Maria protested. "We'll get covered with sand."

"Get out. We've got to get out of this sand pit one way or another."

The man with the dog walked over, stumbling across a rut. "Need help?"

Yeah, 'specially since you and your dog caused this whole problem, thought Maria.

"I'd be much obliged," Eli said. "I'm Eli." He extended his right hand. "On the way to Riverview."

"You're on the wrong road," the man said. "You should of kept going straight back there a ways." He jerked his thumb in the opposite direction.

"I've got to see somebody on this road. That's why I made the detour."

"You have to know this crazy road to drive it," the man said, in slurred speech. "Let me drive. Lived here all my life. I've drove cars out of the sand many a time."

Maria watched Austin walk toward the stranger with his hand outstretched trying to pet the dog's head. He drew back his hand as if the dog were scorching hot.

"That man's drunk," Austin whispered. He tried to get Eli's eye to send a warning that he shouldn't allow the man to get inside the car.

"Can you drive this car?" Eli demanded, ignoring Austin. "Who are you?"

"Luther. S-sure I can drive." Luther didn't wait for permission. He stumbled into the seat. His dog followed him. When the man pushed the gas, the wheels spun, covering Eli with sand. Maria and Austin ran to get away from the flying particles.

From her safe place behind a tree, Maria watched the miniature dog jump over the seat. He climbed up to the rear window, bared his teeth and barked angrily.

"Stop!" yelled Eli. "You're digging in deeper."

Luther paid no heed to Eli's yelling. He kept giving the car more gas. It lurched backward and forward in the ruts, spewing out more sand.

Maria watched Eli standing with his hands on his hips, helpless to take control of the car.

If that don't beat the hens 'a peckin'.

After a long time of rocking the car back and forth, Luther drove it out. He opened the door and stepped out, a big smile covering his face. "I told you I could do it." He closed the door, fastening the dog inside.

"Much obliged," Eli muttered.

Maria suspected the obligation was mingled with a load of anger.

"Shake the sand off your clothes before you get back in," Eli ordered. "I don't want this car full of dirt." Austin and Eli shook the tiny granules from their pants' legs while Maria flapped her red skirt in the breeze. Then they climbed in and Eli started to pull away.

Turning around, Maria saw Luther staggering toward the car, waving at them. Luther started yelling. "Tuffy! I want my dog."

"Luther wants Tuffy," Maria dared to whisper.

"Who's Tuffy?" Eli demanded.

"The dog. He's still in the car," answered Austin, holding Tuffy for Eli to see.

"Throw the dog out," ordered Eli. "I'm through fooling with that mongrel."

Austin held Tuffy with his hands behind the dog's neck so he couldn't bite his fingers. He was about to throw Tuffy out the window, but Maria grabbed Austin's arm. She touched the leather strip tied around Tuffy's neck. He snarled and snapped at her.

"Whoa there! I'm not going to hurt you. Just want to look at what you've got tied around your neck." Holding up an antique-looking locket that had been wired onto the strip, she said, "Look at this. It's got carvings engraved into the heart."

"Hurry up!" Eli shouted.

Apparently, Austin had misgivings over throwing the dog out the window, but hesitantly he tossed out Tuffy. The dog landed on his feet and trotted toward Luther.

Luther grinned, showing black gaps between his teeth. He picked up Tuffy and staggered on in the opposite direction from the car.

"Did you ever hear of a dog named Tuffy?" Maria asked. She giggled.

"Probably means the dog is stubborn," answered Austin. "One time, I had a friend who owned a dog like that one. The dog was named Blackie."

"I like Blackie better," Maria commented. "But I don't really like this black dog. I bet he'd bite you for a little of nothing."

"Hush about that dog. I don't want to hear anymore about him," Eli said. "The subject is closed. I'm in a hurry, 'cause I'm stopping at this house up the road to talk to a girl I know." He pointed toward a rundown house where an attractive young woman sat on the steps. Maria gazed at the pretty girl, dressed in green. The ruffles around her neck, the sleeves, and the bottom of the skirt enhanced her beauty. Blonde hair covered her forehead with bangs that reached almost to her blue eyes. The red color painted on her lips was as bright as the fingernail polish she wore.

Expecting Eli?

After Eli stopped the car and stepped out, he pointed to a clump of trees. "Y'all go over there. I need to talk to Flodell for a few minutes," he said.

Maria shivered when she saw an angry look in his eyes. *Why is he sending us over there?* She shot a questioning look toward Austin. He shrugged his shoulders.

Maria and Austin walked toward the trees. Twigs snapped beneath their feet as they stepped underneath a huge tree. Maria sneaked a peek at Eli and Flodell. They clung to each other in a tight embrace.

He sure changed his feelings when he saw that girl. She is real pretty, though.

Maria's face grew warm with embarrassment. She turned away, hoping Austin didn't see the lovers. Maria was glad to see a squirrel scampering up the tree trunk.

Romantic love is supposed to be done in private, she thought, walking to the tree trunk. She rubbed the rough bark. What looked like a heart carved into the wood caught her attention. Maybe she could take Austin's eyes off the love-struck couple on the porch.

"Look at this," Maria said, smoothing the bark.

"What else?" Austin fussed, stuffing his hands into his pockets. "Look at a dog—look at a drunk Indian—what now?"

"See these initials carved into the tree? Sweethearts must have met here a long time ago." Maria felt her heart quiver in spite of Austin's gruffness.

Will my name ever be carved onto a tree? O. S. loves M. G. Orville Sutton loves Maria Grant.

"Read the stupid names to me," Austin grunted. "It's harebrained to carve names in a tree. I'll bet they're inside a heart."

Maria squinted to read the letters, though Austin's cynical answer caused a pain in her heart. The letters were almost worn away by years of wind and rain beating against them. "Looks like L. D. L. loves L. A. L. And, you're right, there's a heart with arrows running through them. Do you know anybody with those initials: L. D. L. and L. A. L.?"

Austin laughed sarcastically. "Course. Everybody knows people's names starting with those letters. They could belong to anybody."

Maria began to think of girls' names beginning with L. "Levicy, Lillie, . . ."

"What about Lucy? That was my mama's name—Lucy Ann. The initials fit it perfectly."

"Yeah, but those were her first and middle names. What was her last name?" Maria asked.

"Same as mine, Lincoln. My mama is Lucy Ann Lincoln. She thought she was a great Charleston dancer." Austin smiled and rolled his eyes. Then, he crossed his hands on his knees and did a short parody of the Charleston. "She abandoned me to try to make it big in Hollywood. She thought she was good enough to be a hit. More important to me is that she's Sheriff Lucky Lincoln's sister." Austin smiled and straightened a notch taller.

Austin is proud of his uncle, the sheriff.

"Wonder who L. D. L. is?" Austin asked. "I don't know Lucky's middle name, but the two L's stand for his name. I doubt they stand for my pa. I never knew him. I was just five when Mama put me on the bus and sent me to boarding school. Later, I found out she went off to Hollywood with a bunch of dancers. At least, that's what Uncle Lucky told me."

"How did you come to live with Brother Solomon and Watema? Seems like Clear Creek Boarding School is where Brother Solomon was superintendent when Papa finished school."

"He was still superintendent when Jenny Blackwell was going to school there. She found me sleeping under a tree the next morning after I got off the bus. She took me to the cabin and I stayed with Mama—I called her Watema back then—and Caleb until the secret got out that I was living with them.

"Later, Uncle Lucky gave Brother Solomon custody of me. When Watema got married to Brother Solomon, I felt like they were my mama and papa."

Austin glanced toward the house. "Wonder when we'll be leaving?"

Maria looked at the porch, but Eli stood there alone. She watched as he took out a handkerchief and wiped his lips. *Flodell's lipstick?*

Why doesn't he say it's time for us to go?

"You mean Watema isn't you're real mama?" she asked in a loud voice. She covered her mouth when she saw Eli frowning at her. She lowered her voice to ask, "Caleb isn't your real brother then, is he?"

"No, just seems like it. He gave me my nickname, Buck," Austin said. He smiled, and then he looked at the carved heart and letters. Rubbing them, he added, "This could be the initials of my real parents. Who knows?" He glanced toward the porch and nodded toward Flodell who was walking out the door with a bag in her hand. "Looks like we have an extra passenger. She sure looks pretty!"

Maria looked up to see Flodell, who had changed into a fancy purple dress. She had put on another layer of lipstick. Eli motioned that he was ready to leave.

Rubbing her fingers over the carvings one last time, Maria turned to run after Austin as he trotted toward the car. They hurried to climb in the backseat. After Eli helped Flodell in the front, he walked around the car to get in.

"Are you going with us?" Maria asked, leaning over the seat to speak to the pretty girl.

Austin touched Maria's arm and frowned. He put his fingers to his lips, "Sh-h-h."

"I'm glad there's another girl going with us," Maria countered.

Eli scratched the back of his head and cleared his throat. "I'm gonna have to let y'all out up at the main road," he mumbled. "Me and Flodell are gonna go get married."

"What?" yelled Maria. "What about Austin and me?"

"Don't worry about the horses, you just load the wagon," Eli said, turning to face Maria and Austin. "I'll show you which way to go."

"But Eli, do you think that's right to dump them out on the road?" protested Flodell.

"You be quiet, too," he said tersely. He started the motor and turned the car in the direction from which he came.

Maria covered her face and started to cry softly. *Why did we get mixed up with Eli, anyway? That girl had better get away from him. He's mean.*

Austin leaned toward Maria. "Hush. You'll just make things worse." He fumbled for her hand and squeezed it.

I wish Orville was sittin' beside me.

In a few moments, Maria leaned over the front seat and tried to calm her jittery nerves by talking to Flodell.

"You sure will be a beautiful bride. Do you know who's going to marry y'all? My papa's a preacher and he's performed a few weddings."

"That's up to Eli," Flodell answered through trembling lips. "He said he knows a preacher who'll tie the knot for us."

"What's his name, Eli?" Maria asked.

Another angry frown covered Eli's face.

I hope when I get married, my new husband doesn't frown all the time. Will he be Orville?

"Where does your pa live?" Eli asked.

"We live in Durant, but that doesn't matter right now. My pa is gone to a preachers' conference. Oh, no!" she said, covering her mouth.

"What's wrong?" asked Austin.

"Nearly every preacher I know of is at that conference. Wonder who'll marry Eli and Flodell?"

"Don't worry none, Flodell," Eli said. "There's always the Justice of the Peace." He pushed the foot feed and the car spun through the sandy ruts. They rode on in silence.

Maria noticed tears welling in Flodell's eyes and often she dabbed at them. At times, Maria glanced out the window to see if Luther was still walking up the road. Looking for Luther and Tuffy helped to keep her mind off her monstrous problems.

When they reached the main road, Eli stopped the car. Pointing toward the east, he said, "Just follow this road. You'll get to Riverview in a few miles. Get out! Me and Flodell gotta find us a preacher or a Justice of the Peace."

Flodell glanced back at Maria. Tears flowed down her cheeks. Taking in a big breath, she blurted out, "Can I go with y'all?"

Flabbergasted, Maria answered, "Sure, but . . . "

"Then, I'm getting out, too. I'm going with y'all." She grabbed the handle and opened the door. She looked at Eli as if begging him to protest.

Maria searched Eli's face for traces of love and concern, but she found none. Just a cold, heartless stare.

Eli gave Flodell a rough shove, pushing her out. "If that's what you want, good riddance." He tossed out her bag. "Take your stuff with you. I sure don't want it." The engine raced and the car sped away, leaving the trio alone on the roadside.

Chapter Two

"Seems like I smell a skunk in the woodpile," Austin said, staring at Flodell. "Why did you get out? Got cold feet about getting married?"

"A cold heart would be a better way of saying it and it belongs to Eli," Flodell said, covering her face with trembling hands. "He don't love me."

Maria wondered about the real problem Flodell dealt with, but she didn't speak aloud of it. Instead, she looked at the lowering sun and remarked, "We'd better start walking to Riverview. We may have to stay all night with Granny Wade."

About an hour later, the tired youths entered town. Maria led the way to Granny Wade's house. Austin had planned to stay with Uncle Lucky, and Maria wanted to see White Rabbit while she was in town, but because of all the intrusions on the trip they accepted Granny Wade's offer to put them up for the night.

After eating supper, the group sat on the porch to talk a while. Granny said, "Austin, I remember the first time I saw you. You were such a cutie. You came with Louisa when she brought Maria to see her grandpa, but . . .." Her voice trailed off.

"I remember," Austin said. "He was mean and hollering at Louisa, wasn't he?"

Granny Wade's voice carried a hint of sadness. "Yes, it was a heartbreaking day," she agreed. "But in the end, it turned out for the Glory of God. Papa did make things right with God and everybody before he died. That's all that mattered."

"Tell us about Grandpa Wade," Maria begged. "I barely remember him."

"Your grandpa was a highly respected preacher over at our Indian Church," Granny Wade said, pointing toward a grove of trees. "He preached the Gospel and helped lots of people. We even took in a baby who was left on the steps of the church and raised him as our own son."

Pictures danced in Maria's mind of a cozy family laughing and enjoying life as they sat before an open fire. She had heard her mother speak of the good days when she, her sister, and two brothers lived at home. Something dark and sinister like the blow of an axe had split the family apart. Her mother hadn't told about those days. Maria had just heard snatches of conversation when folks thought she was out of earshot.

"We had some trouble in the family and Papa gave up preaching. That's when your other grandpa, Tobias Grant, started preaching. He took Papa's place. He's a good preacher." Granny turned to Maria and asked, "Will y'all be staying for church Sunday? If you do, you can hear him preach."

Maria answered, "No, the preachers' conference will be over. The pastors need to be back home at their churches. We'll *ride the bus* back home this time." She shot a knowing glance at Austin. He smiled in reply.

"Be sure you meet me back here at Granny's in time to catch the bus," Maria said.

Finally, the exhausting day came to an end. Granny let Maria and Flodell sleep in her daughters' bed and Austin slept in her son, Caleb's, bed. Maria had dozed off, when she was awakened by sobs from the other side of the mattress. Should she ask Flodell to tell about her problems or pretend to be asleep?

Best lay here and pretend I'm asleep.

Maria lay awake for a long time, listening to Flodell's sobs. She wondered how she could help this girl, who was not much older than her. Should Maria act like she didn't hear Flodell crying or should she confront her? For the time being, she decided to remain silent.

The next morning, after eating a delicious breakfast of fry bread and honey, Maria and Austin parted company. Maria watched Austin as he walked toward town, headed for the sheriff's office. She turned to Flodell, "Want to walk with me to see my other grandma?" she asked. "I may be staying all night."

Flodell inspected the polish on her fingernails, then finally she answered, "I don't have nowhere else to go, so I'll go with you." She ran inside to grab her bag.

"Come on, Granny. You go with us, too," Maria said, grabbing Granny's hand.

When they passed Doc Coleman's office, Granny stopped for a moment and remarked, "Maria, that's where Sammy worked after he finished school at Clear Creek. He was interested in becoming a medical missionary back then."

"Wonder why Papa didn't become a doctor?"

"He and your ma decided to move to Durant," Granny answered. "He went to college to get the basics before he made a decision about his future. He started preaching around in country churches. Y'all stayed there while Louisa finished college, too. So, Durant became your hometown."

"Does Sammy still like medicine?"

"He's always doctoring us when we get sick," Maria answered.

"Doc taught him how to drive. They went all over the countryside taking care of sick folks. The longer he worked for Doc, the more he liked medicine. Doc was really good to him. Helped pay his way through college."

"I guess Papa really needed Doc's help, because we didn't have much of our own," Maria said. "But since the Great Depression came along, things turned worse. My folks always talk about keeping the wolf away from the door. When I was little, I thought it was a real wolf."

"We all skimped on everything to make both ends meet, but it's better now with President Roosevelt running the country. It's not perfect yet.

"I wanted you to take a good look at Doc's office and get a picture in your mind," Granny added. She pointed to the hitching rail. "That's where Tobias parked the wagon when he brought Sammy to go on the rounds with Doc. Remember Doc's good heart, child."

As the three women walked from Doc's office, Flodell kept turning around looking at the building, as if trying to memorize every detail.

They walked past the drugstore. "I remember getting us ice cream cones there one time when we got off the bus," Maria said. "Most people made phone calls from there, didn't they?"

"They still do. Mostly they call to tell about sick folks or a death in the family," Granny said. After leaving town, they followed the dusty road that lead to Tobias Grant's house. Flodell clung to Granny's arm, as if she didn't want to lose her.

When they drew near to the house, a pack of hounds darted out to greet the visitors. Tobias walked out to call the dogs back. White Rabbit followed him onto the porch to welcome the group and invited them to sit out front with her.

"Tobias, go draw a bucket of water for these travelers. They're hot and tired," White Rabbit suggested.

After everyone had cooled off, Maria started to tell about the drive to Riverview, but didn't get far before she stopped. Did she want to hurt Flodell? She switched to talking about the purpose of the trip.

"Mama and Papa went to a preachers' conference, and sent me to stay with y'all," Maria said, instead. "Austin came with me. He's visiting his uncle, Lucky Lincoln."

"Is Flodell one of your friends from Durant?" White Rabbit asked, smiling at Flodell.

"No, she's a new friend we met along the way. Probably, Papa would say God put her in my path so we can become like sisters."

"I'm glad y'all are hitting it off so well. You need a sister. Too bad you don't have one, at least not yet." White Rabbit turned to speak to Flodell. "Your dress is very pretty. Beautiful enough for a wedding."

"It *was* my wedding dress. Only I didn't get married yesterday like I was supposed to," Flodell said. She jumped from her chair and ran down the steps. She raced to a pine tree and fell against the trunk. Maria watched Flodell bury her face in her hands. Maria hurried to stand with Flodell, touching her shoulder.

"Crying won't help," Maria said. "It'll just make your head hurt."

"I don't care. What's a headache compared to the things I'm going through?"

"I don't know what you're going through, but you can tell me, if you trust me," Maria suggested.

Flodell started crying loudly. "I can't go back home. I don't have no where to go."

"I know you can go somewhere. I'll think about that problem." She rubbed her brow, trying to come up with a solution to Flodell's situation, but she couldn't block out the conversation that was taking place on the porch. She paused to listen.

"What's going on?" White Rabbit asked. "Did I say the wrong thing? I think her dress is beautiful."

"There's something going on we don't know about," Granny Wade confided. She pulled her chair near White Rabbit's. Maria pretended she wasn't listening, but she strained to hear every word. "She's acting like Louisa did before she left for school at Clear Creek."

My mama, Louisa?

"You don't think . . .?" White Rabbit exclaimed.

"I think she has a big problem," Granny Wade said, nodding. "I went into the girls' room to check on them last night and I heard her crying. If she's in trouble, she'll have to tell us. We can't go sticking our noses in other people's business."

"But she'll need help . . ." White Rabbit protested.

What kind of help? Maria wondered.

"I'm prepared to help," Granny Wade said. "My children have all left home, even Caleb. Papa died, and I can lend a hand now when I couldn't have done it earlier . . . after all, your daughter Hallie . . ." Granny lowered her voice.

Maria had to hold her feet in place to keep from running to hear the conversation. She looked toward the porch to see White Rabbit nodding in agreement.

Someday I'll learn about all this.

Maria took Flodell's hand and led her toward the flowerbed. "While we're thinking, let's pick a bouquet for White Rabbit," she said.

"I don't want to pick a bouquet," Flodell said, snatching her hand away. "Bouquets are for happy times. And I sure ain't happy now."

"Even if we're unhappy, we can do something good for somebody else. Come on with me while I pick some flowers." She walked to the flowerbed. She gathered several red zinnias with long stems. She tucked in sprigs from plants with lacy leaves.

We can take the bouquet to the porch and hear the secret, maybe.

Flodell snapped off a purple petunia to stick in her hair. "Are you satisfied? I picked a flower. It matches my wedding dress," she said. More tears streamed down her cheeks.

"I can promise you that one day you will wear the fancy dress to your own wedding," Maria said. She arranged the zinnias and lacy leaves in an attractive way. She added a few pink cosmos to give a subtle hint of color. The young women started walking to the house. Granny Wade looked up and grew quiet.

"We picked you a bouquet," Maria said, handing it to White Rabbit. "And see how the purple petunia matches Flodell's dress?"

"Matches perfect," Granny Wade said, smiling.

A sad smile?

White Rabbit stood to take the bouquet into the house. She looked down at Flodell's bag. "Did you bring another dress?"

"Yes."

"Why don't you come inside with me so you can change clothes?

You need to save that dress for your wedding day. I know a beautiful girl like you will get married soon."

*   *   *

Hours later, Granny Wade and Flodell began to walk back to town.

"Is it okay for me to go home with you, Granny Wade?" Flodell asked. "I want to stay with you." She couldn't explain why, but somehow she felt safe walking along with Granny.

"Of course, child. I need company. White Rabbit and Tobias still have each other, but I don't have no one, not since my husband died," Granny answered.

"Neither do I. I guess that's why I feel so close to you."

Granny slipped her hand through Flodell's arm and lifted her laced high-topped shoe in the air. "We'll march into battle together," she said, laughing. They moved ahead like soldiers for a few steps before slowing down to a normal pace.

Soon, the two women came near Doc's office. "Let's stop here for a minute," Flodell suggested. "You say this is the doctor's office where Maria's pa worked before he left for college?"

"Yes, this is where he grew into manhood, I would say."

"What's Doc's name?"

"He's Doctor Coleman. Really respected around here, like Papa used to be. He's a backbone of the community. He helps people, regardless of whether they have enough money to pay or not. He came to the church the night Papa died. That was both a sad and a happy time. Maybe when we get home, I'll tell you about it."

"I'd like to hear about it," Flodell answered. "I'm ready to go; just wanted to see Doc's office again."

They turned the corner and walked a few yards farther. In a few minutes, they sat in the swing on the front porch to rest a while. Then, Granny stood and said, "You stay out here and rest. I'm going to make us some fry bread and we'll eat bread and honey for supper."

Soon, they were sitting across from each other, while Granny ate pieces of hot fry bread. Flodell fiddled with her bread, pushing it around with her fork before cutting off a small piece. She swallowed it quickly.

"Do you not like fry bread?" Granny asked.

"I like it a lot, but lately I'm having trouble keeping food down," confessed Flodell.

"I've had that same problem," Granny said. "I got real skinny back then."

Flodell felt her heart fluttering. Maybe Granny could give her advice.

"What was wrong with you?"

"Papa caused me a lot of grief. I believe he had too much pride. Oh, I admit he was a powerful preacher. I already told you that. If something happened that would taint his reputation, he acted like a bulldog."

"Like what?"

"A snarling bulldog. I told you we took in a baby we found on the steps of the church. We named him Caleb after a man in the Bible. Caleb had clubfeet, and I guess that caused him to grow up with an ugly outlook on life. He didn't think he could do the same things normal people did, so he took his spite out on Papa and others, too."

"How?"

"The worst thing was when he held a gun to Papa's head, threatening to kill him—"

Flodell gasped and clamped her hand over her mouth. "Not after all you did for him! He couldn't have," she interrupted in a high voice.

"He sure did," Granny said, nodding. "He and Papa stayed all night in that smokehouse." She pointed to the structure. "They were rescued, but Papa kicked Caleb out that same day. It nearly broke my heart. Caleb was like my own son. The clubfeet didn't keep me from loving him." Granny paused to wipe tears from her eyes. "I guess the problem with Caleb and our other children caused Papa to blow up and try to take revenge on everybody. He took it out on me, and after so long a time, I left. I went to stay in Durant with Louisa and Sammy and Maria. Papa was too stubborn to say he was sorry, and so was I.

"While I was away, Papa about starved to death. But in the end, he did come to apologize to the whole family and he died right after that." Granny pulled a handkerchief from her apron pocket and wept softly. "When he apologized, I started life all over. It's turned right side up again."

"I could change a few names and that would be my story. Well, except for being held at gun point and a few other things," Flodell said. Tears streamed down her cheeks. For a few moments, both women wept silently.

After Granny regained her composure, she asked, "Why would a pretty girl like you get kicked out—or was that your problem?"

"My papa is putting pressure on me to do something. If I don't agree to meet his demands, I can't go back home," Flodell said. "That's why I said I don't have no where to go."

"While you're thinking it over, you can stay with me. Is that all right?"

"There's nothing to think over. I can't do what Papa wants me to do, so I'm on my own. For the rest of my life, I guess."

"No, Sis," Granny said, softly. "Your pa will change his mind. It may take years, but he will.

"Can I call you 'Sis'?"

Flodell smiled and nodded. "Sure. My ma calls me sis." She hesitated a moment. "So while you couldn't eat, you fell off a lot?"

"Yeah, I got real poor. After Papa made peace with us and with God, he died. I got fat again. When your problems are solved, you'll probably be able to eat again," Granny said.

When they're solved . . .

"While you stay with me, you can use the bedroom where my two girls slept."

After supper, Flodell and Granny walked into the bedroom. Granny pulled out a drawer to the dresser. "Put your belongings in there," she said. "Be sure to hang up your wedding dress. I know you'll need it some day. You're too pretty to be left alone in this old world."

For the first night in weeks, Flodell relaxed enough to rest with out crying herself to sleep. She had reached a decision. She must return home to get the rest of her worldly possessions to bring to Granny's. Then she would start a new life. Just her and Granny Wade . . . for the time being.

Chapter Three

*M*aria felt like she was lying in a bed of hot ashes. Words like " . . . acting like Louisa . . . ", " . . . after all, your daughter Hallie . . . " kept shoving their way through her mind. She couldn't put them together and come out with a sensible answer. She must ask White Rabbit about these words before she left. Maria guessed Flodell was wrestling with a big problem. She had an idea of what it was. Occasionally, girls at church quit coming for no apparent reason. Whispers about their entanglements with boys flew back and forth behind cupped hands. She'd heard a few of the rumors. She shuddered to think Flodell endured a similar problem.

But my mama, Louisa? She's a strong Christian. My papa is a preacher. I've got to find out more about them while I visit White Rabbit.

At last, she fell asleep.

Maria's struggle during the night caused her to sleep late. While seated at the breakfast table, she heard a knock at the door. White Rabbit hurried into the front room.

"Flodell! What's wrong?"

"Granny Wade told me that maybe Tobias would take me home to get my clothes. Can I talk to him?"

Maria jumped from the table to hurry to the front door. "I'll go with you, Flodell. I'm sure Grandpa will take you home," she ventured. "Won't he, White Rabbit?"

"He *would, but he's already left.* He's gone to work in the corn field," White Rabbit said, wistfully.

Maria watched Flodell stare at the ceiling. A frightened look covered her face.

"What do I do now? Granny Wade was sure Tobias would help me." Tears filled her eyes.

"Don't worry. We'll manage one way or the other," Maria said. "White Rabbit, is there a neighbor who would take us to Flodell's house?"

White Rabbit untied the strings of her apron and pulled it over her head. "We'll find a way. Don't worry. When you finish your breakfast, we'll set out on foot. I know we can get a ride to Flodell's house."

"I'm almost done eating," Maria said. She ran back to the table and stuffed the rest of a piece of fry bread in her mouth. After washing the sticky honey from her hands, she slipped her feet into her black patent leather slippers and smoothed her dress. "Let me brush my hair real quick."

Soon the three women set out on the dusty road toward town. "I know we can find a wagon or a driver to take you home," White Rabbit assured Flodell.

They walked by a rough spot of land beside a ditch. White Rabbit pointed to it and said, "That's the spot where your Grandpa Wade drove his automobile off in the ditch. He was coming out to the house to see Sammy about preaching his first sermon." She laughed aloud. "Those boys! They had at least one bloody fistfight over your Aunt Katrina. That was before Louisa came into our lives."

"Why were they fighting?" Maria asked.

"Over Katrina. They both claimed her."

"How come Papa married my mama, Louisa, then?"

"After he met her, he believed she was just as pretty or prettier than Katrina. He fell in love with her and they got married." She looked away. "Do you have any ideas about who we can get to take us to Flodell's house?"

"Yeah, one idea," Maria answered.

Why did White Rabbit stop talking about my mama?

"If we can find Austin and his uncle, maybe Lucky will take us to Flodell's house," Maria said.

"Oh, that would be so good!" Flodell said, sighing in relief. "I wouldn't worry about a fight if the sheriff could do that."

"That's my plan, as of now," Maria said. The women walked even faster.

*　　*　　*

Later, Sheriff Lucky Lincoln and Austin sat in the front of the car, while Maria, Flodell, and White Rabbit were packed like sardines in a can in the backseat. Tight squeeze or not, they were moving along to Flodell's house to get her clothes.

"Be careful, Lucky," Austin warned, as they rode along. "The sand gets deep along here."

"Who's driving this sheriff's car?" Lucky demanded. He turned to look at Austin. "Who's the sheriff? Who drives all over these roads every day?"

Maria watched Austin cower down in the seat. "You, Sir," Austin whispered.

"That's better," Lucky answered, rubbing his fingernails across his pants and gazing at them. "Just remember, I am the sheriff and have been for the last eleven years. I know my job inside and out. I know which roads I need to pay attention to when I'm driving over them."

Suddenly, the steering wheel started spinning and Lucky fought to regain control of it. He stopped the car and put the gearshift in reverse, shoving his foot on the foot feed. Maria felt like she was going through a torture test as the car jutted forward, then backward at a high rate of speed. The three women held on to each other's arms as they shot back and forth in the seat.

"Why, you . . ." Lucky yelled at the car and beat the steering wheel with both fists. "Why did you bother me while I was driving?" Lucky yelled at Austin. "I was doing fine till you butted in." He slung open the door and gingerly stepped out onto the sand.

Where's Luther and Tuffy?

When Maria thought of the man, she searched the roadside looking for him.

"Do you know a man named Luther?" she whispered to Flodell. "He has a black dog he calls Tuffy."

Flodell nodded. "He lives up the road not far from here. His wife has a white dog, named Teency. "

"Lucky," Maria called. "Let me and Austin go get a man to help us. He's used to driving cars out of the sand. He lives up the road a ways."

"And just who is this expert driver?" Lucky asked.

"His name is Luther and he drove us out of the sand the other day. Can me and Austin go get him?"

"Yeah, yeah, go get the man. I bet he can't do any better than me," Lucky said.

Maria, Austin, and Flodell climbed out of the car and hurried down the road.

"Maria, you be careful," White Rabbit yelled.

Luther's rundown shack was not far down the road. Austin opened the gate to the front yard and led the way up a rock pathway leading to the house. Maria gazed in wonder at the gorgeous flowers growing on either side of the pathway. Standing before the door, she touched one of the velvety red roses growing on the vines of the climbing rose bush. She jumped when a white dog dashed out, wagging its tail.

"Teency," Flodell said. "Come here." Teency jumped into her arms and Flodell smoothed the dog's coat. "I hope Luther is sober enough to drive the sheriff's car. He has a problem with drinking."

She knocked on the door and called, "Are you here, Luther?"

A woman stepped to the door. "Why, Flodell, come in," the lady said, opening the door wider. "Bring your friends in with you."

The bare room showed the woman to be a neat housekeeper. A spotless wooden floor with a rag rug in the center and clean plank wall bore evidence of her persistence to tidiness. Centered on a board on the wall hung a faded picture of Jesus.

Sparse furnishings, but the house is spotless.

"Gracie, this is Austin," Flodell said, pointing to Austin. "The sheriff is his uncle."

"You don't say!" Gracie exclaimed.

Flodell nodded toward Maria. "That's Maria. Our car is stuck in the sand. Is Luther sober enough to drive it out?"

"Good for you, he is," Grace said. "He's broke; can't buy any moonshine. Let me get him." She went to another door and called, "Luther, can you drive a car out of the sand for these people?"

Maria heard a grunt come through the crack in the door.

After a long while, Luther walked into the room, fastening the straps of his blue and white striped overalls. He was barefoot. Tuffy followed at his heels. Tuffy snarled when the saw the visitors, but Luther smiled at the youths and nodded to Grace. "I saw 'em the other day. In the same car?"

"No, this is the sheriff's car," answered Flodell.

A startled look appeared on Luther's face. "But I'm not drunk. Don't have a penny to my name." He pulled his pockets wrong side out. "See?"

"He's not coming after you," Flodell said. "He's bringing me home to get my clothes. I'm—I'm moving out." Her lips trembled as she spoke.

"Oh," Luther responded, and stared at the floor.

"Luther, leave the dogs here and go drive the car out," Grace said. "I'll talk to Flodell while you're gone."

Flodell shook her head. "I don't have time to talk. Maria's granny is in the car waiting for us. Maybe I'll come visit later."

"You can talk a minute," Luther said. "I gotta put on my shoes."

Everyone except Luther walked into the yard while Flodell

explained her dilemma. When Flodell began to cry, Maria took Teency from her arms. "Here, let me have the dog, while you get control of your feelings."

She walked away with Teency and touched the locket fastened onto the strip of leather.

Wonder whose pictures are in this locket?

Gracie came over and touched Maria's hand. "You wondering about the locket?" She reached for the locket and she opened it. She held it up for Maria to read the word "Grace" printed on a piece of paper. The other side had a picture of a baby. "That's me when I was six months old. I had just been named. My parents had a standoff about naming me. Papa held out to name me Grace. Mama wanted me to be Lizzie after her mother. Papa won, and they had my picture taken that day."

"What's in the locket around Tuffy's neck?" Maria asked. She reached toward Tuffy, but jumped back when he snarled and barked angrily.

"Luther's picture," Grace said and laughed. "He doesn't have a story about his name, but I put a picture of him in the locket, so they'd be alike."

"Interesting," Maria said. She glanced at the porch. "Looks like Luther's got his shoes on. We need to go."

Everyone trudged through the sand toward Lucky's car. Luther knew exactly how to maneuver it out of the sand. Soon the passengers were back inside the car, on the way to Flodell's residence. As they approached the house, Flodell started trembling. "Why don't y'all stay in the car? I'll hurry in and get my clothes. Maybe Papa won't cause a fuss, since the sheriff's with me. I hope he's still in bed."

"No, I'm going to the door with you," Lucky said, climbing from the car. "I didn't come out here for nothing. Who is your pa?"

"Boogie Estep. You know him," Flodell said, with certainty.

"Yeah, I do," Lucky twirled the chain from his pocket watch. "I sure do. One false move and he's headed for jail."

Where would Boogie ride? Maria wondered. *Hang on the fender? Somebody might have to stay here out under the trees!*

"I'll knock on the door," Lucky said, walking up the steps. "You stand behind me."

"Ps-s-s-t. Austin," Maria whispered, after Lucky and Flodell reached the porch. "Let's go look at the heart carved in the tree." She pointed toward the trees.

Austin nodded and opened the car door. Maria motioned for White Rabbit to follow them. When they stood before the carved tree, Maria whispered to White Rabbit, "See these initials? We think L. A. L. belongs to Austin's mother. Her name was Lucy Ann Lincoln."

"What's that?" White Rabbit asked, pointing to the initials above them.

"We think they're L. D. L," answered Maria, looking closely.

"Seems to be that," agreed White Rabbit. She rubbed her fingers over the initials. "Those initials could be something else, if you ask me. Seems like the letters are worn."

A new idea. Maria walked to another tree and rubbed the bark. *This would be a good place for my and Orville's initials.* She glanced toward the house. "I think somebody's coming to the door."

Austin and White Rabbit looked at the door. A tousle-haired man, holding onto his trousers with one hand, stepped onto the porch. Maria watched in dismay as the man glared at Flodell. "What you doin' here?" He yelled. "I told you don't come back home without a marriage license in one hand and holdin' onto a husband with the other. I don't see neither one."

The three passengers started sneaking toward the car in time for Maria to hear Lucky clear his throat and say, "That's enough, Boogie. She just wants her clothes. Let her come in and get them. Then we'll leave. Or else . . ."

"Don't worry. We don't want nothin' pertaining to Flodell left here. Go on in, tramp," he snarled. Boogie opened the door wide enough so he didn't touch his daughter when she walked through. "Hurry up," he sneered. "Don't want the likes of you or your stuff on my property."

Lucky shifted from one foot to the other, swinging the chain of his pocket watch around his forefinger. The other hand held onto his pistol. He watched every move Boogie made, like a cat watches a mouse, ready to pounce. If Flodell's pa did anything out of the way, Lucky would make his move. Boogie stood ramrod straight, except to hold up his pants. His pose reminded Maria of a student lined up to march into the schoolhouse.

Maria trembled as she watched the two men, staring down each other. "You think Flodell will get back to the car before they have a fight?" she whispered to White Rabbit.

"Probably. Lucky don't really want a fight. He's just bluffing," White Rabbit answered.

Soon, Flodell came through the door carrying a few dresses. Her mother followed her, crying hysterically. "Don't leave, Sis. Your pa'll forgive you, won't you?"

Boogie drew back his free hand and gave his wife a resounding slap. "Does that answer your stupid question?" he mocked.

The woman covered her face with her hands, sobbing hysterically.

Maria saw Lucky swallow a big gulp of air.

Now's the time to make that arrest.

"Get in the car, everybody. We got to be leaving," Lucky said, pushing Flodell down the steps. "I don't want in the middle of a family squabble. They're the worst kind." He followed Flodell, as she stumbled down the steps clutching her clothes. He turned to face Boogie and his wife. "Y'all work this out on your own. Your daughter is leaving and I say it's just in the nick of time."

The passengers climbed into the car followed by Lucky. He raced the motor, driving away as fast as the car would go. When they were out of sight of the house, he stopped a moment and his head fell onto the steering wheel. "Family squabbles are the worst kind," he repeated. "They'll fight each other, but if I interfere, they'll turn on me.

"I'll stop at Luther's till my heart calms down. Wish he had a swig of that booze left."

Maria's heart did a flip-flop. She wanted to get to know Grace, who looked so loving, but not at the price of Lucky drinking on the job. Grace was pretty, and warm love seemed to radiate from her smile. It sparkled in her eyes. Maybe she could show some of that love to Flodell in her time of deep need.

Lucky parked near the fence at Luther's house. Lucky and Austin crawled out, followed by the backseat passengers who got out to look at the flowers. Lucky walked around the yard whistling. Austin followed his every move.

In a few moments, Grace walked out to visit with them.

Maria smiled at Grace, but was intent on listening to Austin talk to his uncle. "You didn't really mean you wanted a drink of booze, did you? Sheriffs aren't supposed to drink while they're on the job."

"You're right, son. I was just spouting off because my heart was running away with itself. I'm about to calm down now."

"Uncle, yesterday at Flodell's . . . "

"You were there yesterday?" Lucky interrupted sounding like a shrill whistle blowing, stopping the action at an exciting game.

Luther peeked out the door. "What's goin' on? Is something wrong?"

"No," answered the sheriff. "We're just catchin' our breath. We're fine."

"Maybe I should go inside to see what Luther's up to," Grace said. "Take your time. Stay as long as you want to." She walked back to the porch and stepped inside the house.

"What are you talking about? You were there yesterday?" Lucky asked.

"Up at Flodell's, Eli sent me and Maria to go out under the trees and stay while he visited Flodell—" Austin began again.

Maybe I need to help explain, Maria thought. She walked toward the sheriff and his nephew. She noticed Austin looking at the ground and kicking a stone.

"Tell him, Austin. It was your idea," Maria goaded.

"I wasn't going to tell, but to save some money, we paid Eli and rode with him. I heard Eli say he was coming this way, so Maria and I gave him part of our ticket money for a ride."

"I'm all for saving money," Lucky said, "but not when taking risks are involved. Go on. Maria, you're in on this. Tell me more."

"Everything was fine till we got to the road where we turned off today to come to Flodell's." Maria pointed toward the north. "Eli said he needed to see a girl—yeah, it was Flodell—and while they were talking, they decided to get married, I guess. On the way back, Eli let us out at the main road," Maria continued. "We had to walk the rest of the way to Riverview."

"They didn't get married, did they?" Lucky asked.

"I'm afraid Eli is a mean person," Maria confided. "He didn't act nice to Flodell, like other men treat the women they're about to marry. Not the ones who come to our house to get married, anyway. Actually, he pushed her out of the car and drove off."

"I think I'm getting the picture. Her pa is kicking her out, too. Reminds me of other girls who go through hard times like Flodell's going through," Lucky said, staring into a tree. "It happens real often and sometimes I have to help to corral the situation. I don't like that part of this job.

"How are y'all going home? Riding the bus, I hope?"

"Don't worry. I am not catching a ride with a stranger," Maria said. "I'm going by bus."

"Me, too," Austin said.

Lucky walked to the car and motioned for the passengers to follow him. Riding along, Austin seemed restless. Finally, he touched Lucky's arm and asked, "Uncle, do you think anything like that happened to my ma?" His voice was barely audible. "I wonder if a man with the initials L. D. L. is my pa?"

"Why L. D. L.?' Lucky demanded.

"Eli sent us out to that grove of trees while he talked to Flodell. We found one tree with initials carved inside a heart. The top ones could be my mama's initial. L.A. L.—"

"That matches your mama's name. The other initials was—?"

"We think they were L. D. L.," Maria said.

Lucky shook his head. "I don't think that would be your pa. Sorry, son." He cleared his throat. "You're sixteen, ain't you?"

"I am, too," Maria said, hoping he'd let her in on the secret, too.

"I may talk to you tonight when we get home, if I'm not out on a call."

"Thank you, Sir," Austin said, sinking deeper into the car seat.

Maria could almost feel her heart drop into her shoes. Why couldn't she be in on the news?

The rest of the trip to Riverview was a quiet one, except for an occasional sob from Flodell.

Lucky drove to Granny Wade's to let Flodell out.

"I'll visit with you before I leave," Maria promised Flodell.

Soon, White Rabbit and Maria climbed out of Lucky's car. Tobias hurried to meet them. "What happened?" Tobias asked. "I've been looking everywhere for you, *Iskitini*, (Little One)," he said to White Rabbit.

"I'll see to it that Austin's ready to catch the bus tomorrow," Lucky promised as he drove away. "Don't want nothing like this to happen again."

*   *   *

Early the next afternoon, White Rabbit and Maria walked to Granny Wade's. Maria wanted to have enough time to talk to Flodell.

Where will Flodell stay?

Without permission, Maria knew she couldn't bring a stranger into the apartment where her family lived. She, her two grannies, and Flodell needed to have a serious discussion.

Granny Wade and Flodell were drinking tea while they sat in the gently rocking porch swing. When Maria and White Rabbit walked through the gate, Granny stood and asked, "Do y'all want to drink tea with us? Come on, sit down."

"Sure," White Rabbit said, wiping the sweat from her forehead. "It's warm today."

While the four women sipped tea, Maria wondered how to get the conversation going about Flodell's future sleeping quarters. She needn't have worried. Flodell tackled the problem.

"I'm so glad Granny Wade said I can stay with her for a while," Flodell said, looking toward Maria.

"I have a feeling her pa will be sorry for the way he acted and ask her to come back home," Granny Wade said. "She's welcome to stay, though, even if he doesn't come begging her to go with him."

"I won't sit around holding my breath waiting for that to happen," Flodell said. "And even if . . . "

"You might not go back home?" White Rabbit asked.

"I'd have to give it some deep thought before I do."

"Or Eli might come looking for you and want to get married," suggested Maria.

But I hope not.

"I wouldn't touch him with a ten-foot pole," Flodell scoffed "I'm through with him. When he pushed me out of his car; that was the end between us. I'd sooner go back home and face Papa, than to marry him."

"Unless he has a change of heart and trusts the Lord as his Savior," White Rabbit added, hopefully. "That is possible."

"Yeah," said Flodell. "And Red River running out of its bounds during a drought is possible, but probably won't happen."

"Don't get sassy," White Rabbit said and laughed. "With God, 'All things are possible if we only believe'."

"It would take a act of God for all my problems to be solved," Flodell said, sniffing into a handkerchief. "But I know it is possible."

"That's a good beginning," Granny Wade said, and touched Flodell's arm.

Maria felt more relaxed knowing that Flodell would be sleeping snugly in the bed her mama and Katrina used to share. Looking toward the road, she saw Austin walking through the gate.

After they talked a while, the entire group walked to the drugstore to wait for the bus to leave. White Rabbit would walk on home after Maria and Austin boarded the bus.

Maria left, with the promise from Flodell that they'd write letters to one another. She knew she'd see Orville tomorrow perhaps, but she was too tired to think about him. She fell asleep soon after boarding the bus. A while later, Austin shook her shoulder. "I'm getting off at this stop. See you next time you come around."

Missed out on finding out about those initials, she thought.

Chapter Four

"You mean we're moving?" Maria asked in a shrill voice. "Moving where?"

"The District Superintendent said Papa was ready to work in a place where there's no church for the people to worship, like a mission," Mama said. "He said we were moving to Sandy Hill."

"Where's Sandy Hill?" Maria asked. "Will we be leaving everybody we know?"

Even Orville?

"Not really," Sammy said. He smiled and added, "In fact, it's not too far from Riverview. It's new mission work, so there's plenty for me to do. Lots of visiting and meeting the people."

"How soon are we leaving?"

"Real soon," Louisa said. "In time for you to enroll in the new school. I know you don't want to leave the high school at Durant, but you have to."

"I don't like this one bit."

I can't leave Orville.

"A pastor's family has to be open to the Lord's leadership," Sammy said.

"What if I found somebody in Durant to stay with?" Maria looked away, staring at the wall.

"Who, for example?" Louisa asked.

"I don't know. Maybe a preacher's family?"

That's a good idea.

"Do you know how many people want to live with the preacher's—any preacher's—family?" Sammy asked. "That's another challenge to life in a pastor's home."

"I dare you to name some preachers who have kids living with them," Maria said.

"The most obvious one to me is Caleb. Think, Daughter. He lived with my family until Papa drove him off. Now he lives with Brother Solomon," Louisa said.

"Oh, yeah," Maria agreed. She felt herself wilting under the pressure. "But he's a special case. Watema told me he had clubfeet. Then he fell out of a wagon and his legs were hurt too bad to fix."

"His feet were amputated. He got new feet and legs. Yes, he is different," Louisa said. Maria noticed a faraway look in Louisa's eyes. "He was raised as my brother, but because he had clubfeet, Papa treated him different from the rest of us. We had to wait on him, hand and foot. Even with the extra care, he grew up to be bitter. And he took his anger out on all of us."

"He's changed now, right?"

"He changed as much as black is from white," Sammy said. "The Lord did that, but when he got new legs and feet, he started acting better to everybody. He used to be cruel to Watema."

"In what way?" Maria asked.

"He said hateful things to her," Louisa answered. "He was rude and called her bad names. Made fun of her because her two front teeth had been knocked out. She wouldn't stand for it. She got back at him."

"And don't forget about Austin. Brother Solomon and Watema are raising him because his mama put him on a bus and sent him to Clear Creek Boarding School. There are lots of others. I guess that's why the Choctaws have boarding schools for students whose parents need help. Who knows? We may get a child to raise some day."

"Caleb and Austin prove my point," Maria said, wagging her finger back and forth. "I can find a preacher in Durant to stay with and keep going to school here."

"You have parents who love you. Just remember that," Louisa said with finality.

"I think you'll be better satisfied when we move to Sandy Hill," Sammy said.

I'll stay somewhere. Just thinking about Sandy Hill makes me want to puke.

Maria ran to her room to plan her strategy. She'd find a place to stay. She grabbed a sheet of paper and a pencil. She nibbled on the eraser while she mulled over which close friends with whom she might live. In a few minutes she started scribbling down their names. Looking over the list, she shook her head and marked through the girls who had several younger brothers and sisters. No use asking them. After scratching off the names of girls with large families, only three remained.

"Norma Jean Pipkin—too high up for me. She takes tap dance and piano lessons. I know she wouldn't let me stay." Maria sighed. She marked through Norma's name. Finding a family to live with was not going to be easy.

Probably the ones with several kids would be easier to ask.

"Wanda Lou Knipe—she doesn't care about anybody but herself. I know we'd be fighting all the time and her mama would send me packing if I made her precious daughter mad." Maria scratched several lines through her name. Definitely not *Miss Conceited*.

The only name left was Charlotte Elkins, the preacher's daughter. Maria realized Brother Elkins would almost be forced to take her in, since he was always preaching about loving your neighbor as yourself.

Would that be fair? Not really.

Maria wadded the paper and tossed it into the trash. She'd start on a new list tomorrow. She couldn't rest, though. Names kept dancing through her head. She tried to keep them in mind, but at last she wrote down the new ones she'd come up with.

I want to be able to see Orville, at school at least.

The next morning at breakfast Sammy seemed eager to get the move to Sandy Hill started. "I need to go see Brother Elkins and ask him to walk me through the church. One of these days, we may start a building at Sandy Hill."

Maria's heart skipped a beat. She needed to go along to find a place to store her belongings till she found a family to take her in.

"I want to go with you," she said.

Sammy turned to gaze at her quizzically. "For what reason, Daughter? You never have acted interested in church buildings before."

"Aren't two heads better than one?" Maria asked.

"Maybe three," said Louisa. "Why don't we get Sister Elkins and Charlotte and make it a two-family visit? Sister Elkins can tell me how a preacher's wife handles the questions that come up."

"I like that idea," Sammy agreed. "I'll drive over to his house and ask when we can meet at the church. Maria, you need to be ready when he says we should come."

* * *

Later that afternoon, Sammy's family entered the auditorium of the Community Church. Brother and Sister Elkins and Charlotte sat on the back pew waiting. They smiled their welcomes.

The two women sat in the auditorium while they visited. The pastors left to walk through the church, and the two girls roamed from end to end of the building. Charlotte led the way into classrooms, telling Maria which group studied in each room. "What's in here?" Maria asked as they passed a door.

"That's the broom closet," answered Charlotte. "You wouldn't be interested in it."

Yes, I would.

As they walked up and down the hall, Maria knew she'd found a place to hide her personal items, if no girl took her into her home.

"So that's it?" Maria asked when they returned to the auditorium.

"That's it," said Charlotte. She flopped down into the pew beside her mother.

Maria listened as Sister Elkins told Louisa about folks who asked for handouts. "There's always someone in need . . . those with real needs . . . and some who just have wants. You have to pray for wisdom to know which person to give to. Every day someone comes begging for help," she said.

That takes Charlotte's name off the list. I'll have to make another plan. I wonder if Orville can help me.

When the men returned, Sammy seemed exuberant. "I can hardly wait to get started," he said. "We need to go home and begin to pack." He rubbed his hands together.

I'm gonna have to work fast.

At home, Maria hurried to her room and started digging through drawers. She must select necessities to keep with her while she stayed in Durant—a couple of dresses, socks, underwear, the bare minimum. Maybe she could buy an item or two as time went on. She hadn't gotten around to asking Charlotte if she could stay with her. Of course, that decision would have to be made by her parents. From the sound of her mama's words, Sister Elkins didn't want to assist the ones who weren't in real need. Maria felt eliminating Charlotte's name from her list was necessary.

At supper that night, Sammy studied a calendar to decide when to move. "We need to pack most of the things Monday night and be ready to finish loading the beds and other essentials early Tuesday morning. It'll take several hours of slow driving to get to Sandy Hill by nightfall."

"Why don't we go to your folks' house Monday, and we can spend the night with them? Or we could sleep at Mama's," Louisa said, rubbing her fingers over the tablecloth.

Yeah. I would like to see Flodell.

"Then we could go on to Sandy Hill early Tuesday morning. We'd have more time to get the beds set up so we can sleep that first night."

"I like that idea," Maria said, clapping her hands. "I could stay with Flodell at Granny's while y'all go on to White Rabbit's."

"Staying at both places will give us more room to stretch out," Sammy agreed.

"So, what do I plan for?" asked Louisa.

"Plan to spend Monday night with both families," Sammy said.

"Yea! I get to see Flodell," Maria said, jumping up and down.

I've got to do some planning to get my ideas to work.

The next morning, Maria sneaked to the church and hid a few clothes in the broom closet. Closing the door to the church behind her, she breathed easier. She had stashed away two changes of clothes and other essentials. Still, she held her breath; hoping one of her friends would beg her to stay with her family. Thus far, the number remained at zero.

Maria walked to a corner drugstore where she and her friends occasionally met for ice cream. She hoped that several of the girls would be there lounging at a round table, but she found no one. She walked around the block and peeked in the window, but still no close friend was inside the store. After circling the block five times, Maria breathed a sigh of disappointment and started back to the apartment near Southeastern.

As she walked along, she wondered if she had time to get in touch with Austin.

If he met us at Granny Wade's, we could visit a while.

She walked faster, intending to write him a letter and get it in the mail today. Before she wrote the letter, she asked Sammy if they could stop at Green Briar and pick up Austin to ride along.

"That's okay," Sammy agreed. "We might get there by noon and we could eat a plate lunch before we picked him up."

"I think we should take time to visit with Brother Solomon, Watema, and Caleb," Louisa said.

Maria hurried in to write the letter. She planned to spend the night with Granny Wade, and then ride the bus back to Green Briar with

Austin. She'd return to Durant on the same bus. Her heart was beating like a sledgehammer. Would the plan work? She finished the letter and stuffed it into an envelope. After sealing it, she waved the letter at Louisa as she walked through the kitchen. "Going to the post office," she called.

When she returned from the post office, she went to her room to begin packing. As she lifted a blue dress with ruffles around the hem, she sighed.

It's gonna be hard wearing those same old dresses day after day.

Did she really want to stay in school with Orville enough to make big sacrifices?

I can't change horses in the middle of the stream, she thought. *I'm already too deep into this.* Sighing heavily, she folded the blue dress and placed it in a box.

Chapter Five

Maria roused up from her resting position in the back of the car. Louisa was calling to her.

"Time to wake up," she said. "We're almost to Green Briar."

In a few minutes, Sammy stopped the car in front of the freshly painted white house the school provided for the superintendent and his family. Brother Solomon stood at the door to welcome Sammy's family. He held it open for Watema to walk through, followed by Caleb, who held tightly to his walking stick.

The men shook hands. Watema welcomed Louisa.

"Everybody come in," Watema said. "I cooked dinner for y'all so you'll be strong enough to unload your furniture. Come on in."

"We didn't expect that," Louisa said. "We were going to buy a plate lunch in town."

"Don't be silly," Watema said. Jokingly, she slapped at Louisa's arm. "You know better than that."

Everyone walked into the living room and sat for a few minutes while White Rabbit helped Watema set the table. Maria and Austin walked back to the yard to stand under the pine trees.

"So, do you want to go with us to Riverview?" Maria asked.

Austin nodded.

"Good," Maria said. "I'm staying with Granny Wade tonight and

I thought we could visit with Flodell. So you've made up your mind about coming with us?"

Austin frowned and brushed at his hair. "Yeah. I want to go, but so does Caleb."

How will we all pack into the car?

"He wants to go see Granny Wade," Austin explained. "I don't think there's enough room for all of us to fit into the car. I wanted to see Uncle Lucky and ask him about the initials on the tree. He was out on duty that night he said he'd talk to me."

"So you didn't get to ask about the initials?"

Silently, Austin shook his head.

"Well, I know Caleb wants to visit with Granny Wade since she raised him like he was her own," Maria admitted. "We can't blame him for wanting to go."

I could stay with Watema and give my place to Caleb. Or we could take turns sitting in the trailer with the furniture. Or one of us could ride the bus or train.

"There's lots of choices to pick from," Maria added. "Why, right now I can think of three different ways of you getting to go to Riverview."

"Name one," challenged Austin.

"I could stay here with Watema . . . "

"Then we can't talk to each other," Austin objected.

"You and me can ride the bus or the train, or . . ." Maria giggled. She poked Austin in the ribs. "Or we can hitch a ride. Maybe Eli is around some place."

"You've got to be crazy!" Austin shouted, cracking his knuckles. "You don't mean catch a ride, do you?"

"That was puredee jesting," Maria said. "One of us could catch the bus, though."

"Let's bring it up at the table," Austin said. He pointed toward the front porch where Watema stood waving toward them.

After Sammy said grace over the meal, everyone started filling his plate with *tafula* (boiled hominy), sweet potatoes, and pork.

Maria swallowed a few bites of food before she broached the subject of Caleb going to Riverview with them. "Only problem: there's not enough room for all of us to ride in the car," she concluded.

"I didn't know you'd be so loaded," Caleb said. "I don't have to go."

Brother Solomon cleared his throat. "I think I have the solution, if Watema agrees. Austin and Caleb can stay with y'all at Riverview. I'll take Watema to Valliant for a visit to the park."

Watema gasped and covered her face with her apron. "You don't mean it. Back where we got married?" she asked, peeking around the apron.

"How well I remember your wedding at the park," Sammy said. He laughed boisterously. "My first wedding—I was more frightened than the bride or the groom, but I made it through the ceremony. And you're still married."

Maria watched Brother Solomon reach for Watema's hand and squeeze it. "That's right, Sammy. We're still married and happier than ever. Why don't we divide up and ride in two cars to Riverview? How does that sound, Watema?"

"Good. Can I ride with you?"

"We don't want to separate y'all, after all the years it took to get you together," Sammy said. "Sounds good to me. Keep husband and wife together. The ones who are with me need to leave soon, because I'll drive slower pulling the load of furniture."

"Don't you mean, keep '*husbands and wives*' together?" Louisa teased.

"Of course, you must ride with me," Sammy said. "So now, Austin, Caleb, and Maria need to decide which cars they're riding in and we'll have that settled."

"I'll ride with Mama and Papa," Caleb said. "So, everything's done."

*   *   *

Hours later, Maria, Flodell, Caleb, and Austin sat at the kitchen table with Granny Wade. The room reverberated with laughter.

I'm glad Flodell feels like laughing, Maria thought. With her forefinger, she traced the red and white squares on the checkered tablecloth.

"Caleb, I'm sure glad you came to visit me. It's thrilling to see you walking in on two good feet," Granny said. Maria watched Granny's hands tremble as she pulled a handkerchief from her apron pocket. "I know you were always tied down because of those awful clubfeet."

"I couldn't do nothing because of having to get around on crutches. Now all I need is the hickory walking stick I carved," Caleb responded. "I know it was the Lord's Will that I got run over by the wagon and had to have my feet and part of my legs amputated."

Maria's heart nearly jumped out of her chest at Caleb's words. She knew her misbehavior had caused the horses to run away with the wagon. She was just a little girl when she had slipped off from the cabin when Louisa had told her to stay put.

But I was only five. I didn't know the horses would stampede when I tried to stop the wagon, Maria thought.

"While I was in the hospital at Talihina, Brother Solomon heard about a woman who had her clubfeet cut off on purpose, so she could get artificial legs and feet. Papa really pushed me to get them for my stumps."

"That happened when I was five years old," Maria said. "I caused the whole thing because I was headstrong." She turned to Caleb, and touched his arm. "I'm sorry, but it turned out for the best, didn't it?"

"Yeah, for both of us. I knew if you got run over by the horses and wagon you'd be killed," Caleb said. "I couldn't take a chance on that happening."

"Mama says I was as stubborn as a mule," Maria said, "but for once, it turned out to be worthwhile."

"You're right. Now I have to take it slow, but I can do almost anything anybody else can."

"Is this the man you've been telling me about, Granny?" asked Flodell.

"He's the one. He was raised as if he was one of our own children."

"Now Caleb and me are like blood brothers," Austin said, softly. "Our mothers threw both of us away, you might say. But goodhearted people took us in."

"Like our Lord does. He takes all who accept Him into His family," Granny said.

"My mama says she was forced to give me away," Caleb said. "I believe her."

"Watema fought hard to keep you," Granny said, "but you had a mean-hearted uncle who forced her to take you elsewhere to live. Which reminds me, Maria, are Sammy and Louisa moving to a new church?"

"I don't think there's a church at Sandy Hill, but Papa will do mission work trying to start one," Maria answered.

I won't be in on it. I'll be in Durant getting to see Orville at school everyday.

"That's what he always wanted to do," Granny said. "Except, he wanted to help sick people, too."

"There's always plenty of sick folks around," Maria said. "He'll probably help them since he's good at doctoring people."

After a while Austin stood, ready to visit Uncle Lucky for the night. "Mama and Papa are gone to Valliant on a trip while I visit Lucky. They'll come back through to pick up me and Caleb. I'll be somewhere around Uncle Lucky's office while I'm here."

"I'll go with you to the gate," Maria said, rising to follow Austin. She must let him know she planned to return with him. At the edge of the yard, Maria whispered to him. "I'm riding back with y'all. So don't run off and leave me. I'll meet you here at Granny's."

"But why? Your family is moving to Sandy Hill. Where will you stay?"

"I'll tell you about it later. Just trust me," Maria said, pushing him on.

*　　*　　*

Austin left Granny's house, his mind filled with questions.

What is Maria up to now? Does she want to go to Green Briar School or back to Durant?

He shook his head in dismay. That girl always did have a hankering to stick her finger in the pie and see what flavor it was. After burning her finger or getting her hands slapped so often, it seemed like she'd learn her lesson before long.

Maybe I can help teach her a lesson.

Instead of heading toward Uncle Lucky's house, Austin circled back and walked toward Tobias' place. It wouldn't hurt to let Louisa and Sammy in on Maria's secret plans. No telling what she intended to do.

Run away and get married?

He'd never heard Maria speak of having a feller, but no one knew about girls these days. Some at Green Briar left to visit their parents and never returned.

Sure hope she's not about to get married. She's too smart to quit school. But it's none of my business.

Austin stopped in the middle of the dirt road, debating whether he should meddle or let Maria make her own bed.

Right. It's none of my business.

He turned around and started back to Uncle Lucky's place. A large black cat jumped out of the bushes in front of Austin. He stopped in his tracks. *Was that a black panther?* Black panthers scared him to death. All his life he'd heard older men tell that the big cats sounded like women screaming.

He started to rush on toward Lucky's. Or was it closer to go on to Tobias' house? He spun around and started running toward Tobias'. Give the panther time to be far away by the time he returned.

He ran till he was out of breath, then, he walked as fast as he could. He needed to get back to town before too late.

He breathed a sigh of relief when he spied the flickering of a coal oil lamp shining through the window. A car was parked in the yard with a trailer fastened to it. At least Sammy was still here, but how did Austin tell Sam about Maria without it seeming he was butting into someone else's business? He'd jump in at the right moment. One was sure to come up. He ran up the steps and knocked on the door. Tobias answered.

"Austin!" Tobias exclaimed. "Is everything all right? Anybody sick?" He opened the door wider.

"What's going on?" Sammy asked, rising from his chair. He raked his hands through his thick black hair.

"Is something wrong with Mama?" Louisa asked, rising from her chair.

"Nothing's wrong . . . yet," Austin answered, taking a deep breath. "Let me in. I think I saw a black panther up the road a ways. He scared me. I need to catch my breath."

Tobias laughed. "You probably saw Shadow. He prowls around these parts a lot. He doesn't have any teeth. He can't bite."

"Yeah, but does he have claws?" Austin asked.

"Sure. That's how he tears his food into little bites," White Rabbit said. She looked at Louisa and winked. "You're safe. Rest a minute. Tell us what brings you out our way. I thought you'd be visiting Sheriff Lincoln."

"I may be sticking my nose into somebody's business, but I feel like I need to tell you what Maria said to me before I left Granny Wade's house. So set back down and I'll tell you what I know." He turned to address Louisa. "Is there a reason Maria won't be moving to Sandy Hill with y'all?"

Louisa put her hand over her heart. "Oh, I'm sure glad no one is hurt or sick. You had me scared." She turned to Sammy. "Do you want to tell everybody about Maria's latest pigheaded idea?"

Sammy nodded in agreement. He cleared his throat and spoke. "Maria wants to keep going to school in Durant, that's all."

"Why, that's impossible," White Rabbit exclaimed. "You can't move off and leave her."

"With Maria?" Louisa said, and sighed deeply. "When she gets her head set on an idea, you can't get her to change her mind. It's like pulling teeth. We went round and round about her staying with a family in Durant. Sam and I said, 'No!'"

"She's tried to get us to let her stay with just about anybody who lives there, but we didn't agree with her. We want her to move with us," Sammy said. "Finally, I had to put my foot down. She has to move with us. What's she up to now?"

How do I tell them differently?

"When I was leaving Granny's house while ago, Maria came out into the yard and told me she wanted to go back with me and Caleb. I think she's gonna try to go back to Durant to stay."

"That obstinate girl! Will she never learn she can't have her way all the time?" White Rabbit exclaimed.

"She'll learn," Louisa said, "but I'm afraid it will be too late."

Austin shuffled his feet and gazed at a picture hanging on the wall. Should he leave and let Maria's parents take over? Probably.

"You think that panther is gone on his way by now?" he asked.

"Yeah. He's on over at the creek getting a drink by now," Tobias answered.

Austin stood, and reached out to shake the hands of the men. "Then I'll leave. You can decide what to do."

"Thank you, Austin," Louisa said.

"Let her ride with y'all," Sammy said. "We'll decide how to handle the situation in her best interest. Thanks again."

"Sam! You don't mean that!" Louisa protested.

"If we aren't there to stop her, just take her with you," Sammy said.

"Okay," Austin said, walking out into the night. At least he had done his duty. How Maria's parents handled the problem was their business. His business was to keep an eye out for a toothless panther called Shadow.

Chapter Six

$\mathcal{L}$ouisa stared at the closed door. Had she heard Sammy correctly? Had he told Austin to let Maria ride with them to Green Briar?

"What did you mean, Sam?" Louisa demanded, holding onto the edge of the chair, to keep from rushing toward him.

"Just what I said," Sammy declared, evenly. "Let Maria go on in the car with Brother Solomon and Watema. If there's enough room, that is. I think this is a perfect time for that girl to learn a lesson."

"But you know we've tried to think of even one family who would let her stay with them this school year," Louisa protested. "We haven't come up with a single person."

"That might help her decide to come home even quicker," Sam said. He rose from his chair to walk toward Louisa. He took her hand and looked deeply into her black eyes. "Let me handle this, okay? You're too close to Maria to think straight. Maybe I can keep a clear head."

He doesn't know how I feel. He's not her papa. I'm all she has.

Lousia's conscience reminded her that Maria's biological father was alive and well. The sixteen-year-old wasn't aware of who her father was. Often, Louisa felt as if she bore the burden of parenting alone. Sammy was an excellent father; no doubt about that, but Maria wasn't his daughter.

"I guess I'll have to trust you," Louisa replied, clinging to his hand.

Tears stung her eyes and she tried to smile. "That girl is too headstrong for her own good! She's like her papa used to be before Jesus came into his life."

"He was a challenge," Tobias agreed.

After they went to bed, Louisa and Sammy discussed how to handle the latest escapade Maria was about to dive into.

"Do I have this straight?" Louisa asked. "Does Maria think she can ride back with Austin and them back to Green Briar . . . then go on to Durant from there?"

"That's the way I heard Austin explain it," Sammy answered. "She wants to go to Durant and attend high school there. There's probably some boy she'd like to be around. Why don't we just play along? She'll come begging in a few days. Hopefully, like the Prodigal Son returned to his father."

"And you'll be the father, welcoming her back into the family?"

Louisa heard Sammy sigh. "Don't you know I love Maria as much as if she was mine? I held her in my arms before you did. We were bonded together from her birth," he said. He gave Louisa a reassuring hug. "I'll welcome her back. You know that, but when we leave tomorrow for Sandy Hill, we'll need to act like we're swallowing every thing she tells us, hook, line, and sinker."

"I hope I can do this without crying," Louisa said.

*   *   *

Maria could not fall asleep. She kept thinking of reasons to leave for Durant before her parents arrived. Maybe Brother Solomon and Watema would come for Austin sooner than Sammy came to get her. If that happened, she had no worries about making excuses. Just in case her parents came first, she could say she forgot to turn in the clarinet she played in band. Oh, Mama already knew that the band instruments were checked in at the end of school. *But,* Mama didn't know if she had turned in the books due at the library. Yes, she would say she had failed to turn in books due at the public library. *A lie*. Every excuse she thought of was a bald-faced lie.

Maybe it won't hurt to tell one white lie. I can make it right later.

She turned over to go to sleep. She pulled the covers around her neck and closed her eyes. A vision of the broom closet at the church danced before her eyes. Remembering the musty, oily smell in the closet made her throat tickle and she stifled a cough. Sleeping in the closet was going to be as hard as resting while hanging onto a limb. Just then, a noise in the night caused her to jump.

Did I wake up Flodell?

She touched Flodell's shoulder. "You awake? If you are, I want to talk."

"Yes, I'm still awake," Flodell answered drowsily. "What's your problem? Not much, if you ask me. You don't know nothin' about real problems."

"I don't? Well, I'll bet you don't know how lucky you are, not to have your parents breathing down your neck all time," Maria said. "They let you leave home without a big fight."

"You've got that all wrong," Flodell said. "They, or at least Papa, forced me to leave home. You saw what happened. Papa told me to leave—good riddance! I know Mama wanted me to stay, but she won't dare stand up to Papa. I'd dance for joy, if my parents cared like yours do. I'd be home in my own bed, even if the mattress is lumpy."

"You think I'm lucky because they keep me tied to their apron strings?"

"If Mama and Papa had cared for me like yours do, I wouldn't be in the pickle I'm in today," Flodell said.

"What kind of pickle are you in, besides having to leave home?"

I hope it's not what I think.

Flodell started to sob so heavily the bed shook. "You don't know? Granny ain't told you that—that—I'm—I'm in a family way?"

That's what I thought.

"Oh, no!" Maria said, trying to keep her voice low. "Granny

hasn't said a word. Yes, your problem is bigger than mine. What are you going to do?"

"Who knows? I can't go home." Flodell's sobbing deepened, and the mattress shook like a cat was trapped inside it, trying to claw its way out.

Maria rubbed Flodell's quavering shoulders, trying to comfort her. "I'm sorry. I shouldn't have bothered you. Can you go back to sleep?"

"Yeah. I cry myself to sleep nearly every night."

Maria lay awake for a long time, trying to decide on a solution to Flodell's dilemma. Now three big problems stared her in the face. How would she get back to Durant without her parents' knowledge; where would she live when she arrived; and how could she help Flodell with her predicament? Could the solution to all three questions be found with one great big answer? A wave of despair washed over her.

I can't even solve one problem. Be real.

Mentally, Maria tried to count the money she had in her purse. She had to pay the bus fare to Durant and save some for meals. She'd need to eat with friends quite often, if they invited her over. And she should go to church every time a meal was served. Roast pig and all.

Early in the morning, she would ask Flodell to walk with her to the drugstore. They'd stay there until Mama and Papa had left Riverview. Then she'd be footloose and fancy-free. At last, she drifted off to sleep.

*   *   *

Louisa awoke with a start. She shook Sammy to awaken him. When he realized how late it was, he leaped out of bed.

"Mama, why didn't you wake us up?" Sammy complained, when he stumbled into the kitchen.

"You were tired and needed the rest," White Rabbit responded. "Why don't y'all go to the new church and look around today? You're late starting out, so leave the furniture here and come back to spend the night."

"I think that's a good idea, White Rabbit," said Louisa.

Sammy nodded in agreement. "We can go look around and then tomorrow we'll know exactly where to take the furniture."

Louisa and Sammy lingered over the breakfast White Rabbit had prepared. While White Rabbit and Louisa were drinking another cup of coffee, Sammy and Tobias went to the car to unhitch the trailer. After a while the couple went to the car and said their good-byes. Sammy leaned out the window to say, "We'll be back before dark, I hope."

Louisa bent forward toward Sammy's window. "If Maria comes out today, act as if you don't know she's planning to ride back to Durant. If things don't work out, she could get desperate enough to come stay with you." She felt tears slipping down her cheeks.

"Sammy, let's go before I start to cry," she whispered.

A short distance up the road, they entered Riverview. When Sammy drove past Doc's office, he slowed to a halt. "I learned a lot the summer I worked with Doc Coleman. He was a good example for me. I need to visit him while we're living this close to him."

"But no visit today," Louisa said.

Sammy pressed the foot feed and sped on toward Granny Wade's house. "Pretend you don't know anything," he reminded Louisa.

The couple crawled from the car and hurried toward the porch. Granny met them at the door. "Come on in. I fixed a bite for you," she said.

"Sorry, Mama," Louisa said. "We overslept and all we want to do is pick up Maria and be on our way. I wish we had time to visit, but now that we live near you, we'll visit real often. Where's Maria?" She walked into the room where she and Katrina used to sleep. The bed was tousled but no one slept there.

"Where's Maria?" Louisa repeated, from the bedroom.

"She and Flodell went for a walk after breakfast," Granny said. "And Caleb went down town to see some of his friends."

"What do we do now, Louisa?" Sammy asked. "Go off and leave her—wait for her to return—sit down and drink a cup of coffee, or what?"

"Let's drink coffee while we wait for Maria to come back," Louisa answered. "Our plans have changed, Mama. We slept too late, so today we're just going to be looking around. We'll come back tomorrow and get the furniture and Maria. But we need to get on the road to Sandy Hill pretty soon."

They sat at the kitchen table and savored the coffee. Though they sipped slowly and enjoyed the visit with Granny Wade, Maria did not put in an appearance.

Sammy walked to the cabinet where the granite washbasin and a bucket of water sat. "We've got to go," he said to Louisa, while he washed and dried his hands. "Granny, take care of Maria. We'll come back and get her tomorrow. We're going to look around today." He walked out onto the porch and started toward the car.

When Louisa hugged Granny, she whispered in her ear. "We're not worried about Maria. Just take care of her. She'll enjoy visiting with Flodell." Louisa ran toward the car and waved to her mama. She opened the car door and jumped inside. "Hurry, so Mama won't see me crying."

As soon as they were out of sight, Louisa started sobbing. "What has my little girl done now?" she asked. "I have some idea of how Mama felt when I went off all alone to Clear Creek Boarding School."

"Maria's situation is much different from yours, Sweet Wife. She's just stubborn," Sammy said, patting her leg.

He drove slowly by Doc's office again. He sped up as he drove farther down the street, then he stopped in front of the drugstore while he waited for an oncoming car.

"We're on our way to start a new mission. Remember, God will take care of Sandy Hill and God will take care of Maria." He sighed deeply, and then added, "I admit I'm concerned about her, but we'll have to pray all the time about her safekeeping."

"We sure will," Louisa said.

Sammy pushed the foot feed. The young couple started toward Sandy Hill and a mission with God.

*   *   *

Maria let out a deep sigh of relief. Mama and Papa just drove by and she was sure they didn't have the foggiest notion that she and Flodell sat at a round table inside the drugstore. "It's safe to go back to Granny Wade's now," Maria said, rising from the chair. "Let's get started."

Flodell reached for Maria's arm, pulling her back into the chair. "Just a minute. Where can we go to talk so no one will bother us?"

"I tried to talk last night, but you got to crying."

"I feel better now. I think now I can talk and not cry so much."

"Maybe we ought to go by the sheriff's office first and see when Austin expects Brother Solomon to pick him up. And me, too."

After a stop at Sheriff Lincoln's, Maria felt easier. Brother Solomon wouldn't be coming by till tomorrow. She and Flodell could visit for as long as they wished. And make lots of plans.

"Why don't we just go back to Granny's and talk in your room?"

"Okay. I'll try not to cry."

Granny was walking down the porch steps when Maria opened the gate to enter. "Why, girls, where have y'all been? Maria, your parents have already left but they said they'd be back to get you tomorrow."

A dart of fear stabbed Maria's heart. How much longer did she have to hide out before she left for Durant? She tried to control the quivering of her lips and curve her mouth into a smile. "Are you going somewhere, Granny? I see you have your purse with you."

"Yes. There's a Ladies' Society Meeting over at the church. I didn't know where you two had gone. If it's okay with you, I'll go on. I'll be back in about a hour or so."

"I'll be here all day, I guess. So, go ahead." Maria smiled knowingly at Flodell. *We can talk without anybody interrupting us,* she thought. "Bye, Granny."

The two girls went into Flodell's room and flopped onto the bed. Flodell leaned on one elbow, and examined the red polish on her fingernails. "If you were in my shoes, how would you handle this? I know I'm older than you, but maybe you can tell me what to do," Flodell ventured.

If my pa kicked me out of the house and I was in a family way, what would I do?

Maria pulled a long length of hair near her face and pretended to be looking for dead ends. She took her time looking at a few strands at a time.

"What would you do, I asked?" Flodell repeated. She grabbed the hank of hair from Maria's hand, pulling it from her face. "Don't be afraid to look at me."

How dare she pull my hair? Maria stuck her face in front of Flodell's. "I'm not afraid to look at you," she said, evenly. "I just want to think before I answer. This is a big decision for you to make. There are two lives involved in this problem."

Flodell's eyes filled with tears. Through trembling lips she whispered, "I think about it all the time."

Maria felt her anger soften. "I'm sure you do," she answered gently. "I'll leave you alone for a minute or two. I'll be back in a little bit." She rose from the bed and walked into the front room to think about Flodell's problem. She looked at the faded wallpaper on which pictures were displayed. She walked closer to examine the four pictures. She recognized the two attractive girls—her mama and her mama's younger sister, Katrina. The smiling young men were her mama's older brother, Levi, and Caleb. Something about Caleb caught her attention. She gasped when she realized that his smile looked so much like hers. Goose bumps covered her arms as she studied his features.

That picture was probably taken when he was about the same age as I am, and we would pass for brother and sister. One front tooth laps over the other one just like mine does.

She touched the lapping tooth to make sure it still covered the other one. It did! She ran from the room. The resemblance brought uncomfortable thoughts to her mind. Why did they look so much alike? She walked back to flop down beside Flodell.

"Where'd you go?"

"Just thinking about what I'd do if I were in your shoes." *A lie.* "I'd probably do about the same as I plan to do now. I'm going back to Durant to go to high school there. I don't have a family to room with yet, so I'm out on a limb just like you."

"But where will you stay?"

"As of now, I'm going to hide out in a broom closet at a church. It smells oily and dusty, but that's the price I have to pay if I want to go back to school there."

"Don't you think you're cutting off your nose to spite your face?"

"Not really. I *want* to go to school in Durant," Maria declared. "I don't want to move out to some place that doesn't even have a church."

"No church? That don't make sense. Are you sure it's not because of a boy?" Flodell searched Maria's eyes. "I'll tell you, they ain't worth the price."

"No, a boy is not involved in this," Maria said, turning away. *Another lie.* "If one was, I'd ask his parents to let me live with them." *Maybe I'll do that.* She reached for a pillow to tuck under her head. "I've heard of homes for girls in trouble to live in. Have you thought about that?"

"What kind of homes?"

"They're usually sponsored by big city churches. I don't think you could move to Tulsa or Dallas to live in one, though.

"Do you have any kinfolks you could go stay with? That sounds more likely to solve your problems."

"If Papa heard of that, I figure he'd get in touch with them and forbid them to keep me."

"What about going to a boarding school and staying in the dairy barn or one of the buildings on the grounds?"

"And going out looking for food after the students went to bed?" Flodell countered. "Sounds scary to me. But not as scary as the story Granny Wade told me. It really sounds possible, if I could find the cabin." Flodell pulled out the other pillow and rested her head on it.

"Tell me about it. If it sounds like you could do it, maybe we can use it to help solve your worries."

"Well," Flodell said, pushing the pillow in a more comfortable position, "Granny knew a girl who was in a family way, like me. The girl didn't want to disgrace her family, so she pretended to go away to boarding school."

"That's an idea. What grade would you be in?"

"Twelfth grade . . . this girl found out about a cabin that was close to the boarding school. She told her parents she was going to school, but instead, she lived in the cabin. All alone."

I wonder if there's a shed or a cabin I could stay in at Durant.

"As the time got close for the baby to arrive, the girl panicked and sent word to her sister to see if she could find somebody at the school to come birth the baby. I'll bet she was scared, don't you? That's what I'm worried about."

"Did she find a student?" Maria asked.

"Yeah. But the girl had to sneak off from school to find the cabin. When she didn't come back to class, a search party was organized to find her. It must have been awful for both girls. One girl about to have a baby and the other one didn't know nothin' about birthing babies."

Maria felt a shiver run up her spine. Whoever those girls were, they were brave. She sure didn't want to get involved in birthing babies—oh no, not Flodell's! Is this what Flodell had in mind by telling her the story?

"You're not trying to tell me something, are you?" She rose up on an elbow and stared at Flodell. "You don't want me to birth your baby, do you?"

Maria watched Flodell burst out laughing. "Not quite! I'm just telling you the story Granny told me. How this girl respected her family so much she hid out in a cabin."

"So how did it all turn out? Did the baby live?" Maria asked.

Flodell nodded. "According to Granny, the baby lived. The girl with the baby married the brother of the girl who birthed her baby and they lived happily ever after. Wish I could say that about myself."

Tears formed in Flodell's eyes and she started to cry softly. "What am I gonna do? I can't ask Granny to keep me from now on."

"If I wasn't planning on living in a closet, I'd take you with me to Durant," Maria said. She reached over to hug Flodell. "We're both in hot water."

Maria lay back, trying to find answers to her and Flodell's problems. In a few minutes, she felt her eyelids drooping. She needed sleep.

"Right now, while I'm resting on Mama's old bed, I think I'll take a nap. Remember, I didn't sleep much last night? Somebody spent a lot of time crying." Maria curled up to go to sleep. "I've heard Papa preach on a verse that says 'All things work together for good . . .' but I can't remember the rest of it. Maybe all things will work out for good for you and me."

In a few minutes, Maria heard Flodell's rhythmic breathing. She knew the poor girl had fallen asleep. When Maria closed her eyes, she kept seeing a cabin surrounded by tall pines. A girl wandered around frantically searching for the building. Seems like she had seen a cabin like that before. It looked so familiar.

Chapter Seven

Louisa and Sammy breathed simultaneously sighs of relief when Sammy pulled onto the main road, leaving Riverview. Louisa smiled through her tears and said, "We made it! Oh, I'm glad we were able to get away without a word fight."

Sammy touched Louisa's hand, trying to comfort her. "We still have the battle on our hands. I told Granny we'd be back tomorrow to get Maria."

"Yeah. And I am not looking forward to butting heads with her."

Sammy reached into his shirt pocket to pull out a wrinkled scrap of paper. "Right now, our problem is finding Sandy Hill. Read the directions to me and tell me which way to turn."

Louisa nodded and began reading the paper. "About three miles up the road, turn south onto a dirt road. So that's not hard."

When Sammy pulled onto the road leading south, he expelled a long breath. "Looks like this is nothing more than a sandy pig trail," he muttered. "I've got to be careful with my driving."

Louisa sat in a frozen position, trying to keep still while Sammy drove through the sandy ruts. Would the trail dwindle to nothing before they got to Sandy Hill? "What will you do if the road ends before we get there?" she asked.

Sammy smiled. In mock alarm he asked, "Now, Louisa, does that sound optimistic for the pastor's wife who's beginning her role in a new community? Where's your faith, Sweet Wife?" He patted her hand gently.

Louisa opened the paper to read further directions. "I can't read this," she complained. She turned it sideways, up and down, but couldn't figure out the smudged words. "What will we do?"

"We'll stop at the first house we come to. I'm sure the folks around here will be able to give us directions." Sammy pointed toward the plum trees and berry vines growing beside the trail. "I'd call this the Garden of Eden, if I named it."

"Those plums look good. We may have to stop and pick some to make a plum cobbler for dinner."

"H-m-m-m. I guess we could do that."

What have we got ourselves into? Louisa wondered.

The car clunked along with the wheels spinning through the ruts. "Sure hope another car doesn't come down the road. I couldn't pull over without burying up in the sand."

"If we do meet another car, y'all will have to share the road someway," Louisa said.

"Let's hope so."

Louisa kept her eyes glued to the sides of the trail, hoping to see a house. She believed she'd feel more at ease if she knew where Sammy was headed. He continued to drive pass plum thickets and berry vines. "When we get settled, I could make plum jelly," Louisa commented.

"Sure would be good with fry bread," Sammy mumbled, in an unconcerned way.

In the distance, Louisa saw a dilapidated building. Her heart skipped a beat. A house, perhaps? In the yard grew lush green plants and blooms of vibrant colors surrounded by a white picket fence. Someone lived there! They tended the plants. "Look, Sam. Do you think a family lives in that house?"

"We'll find out soon enough," Sammy answered. "We're stopping here to ask for directions." He drove the car to the edge of the yard.

Getting out, he said to Louisa, "You come with me. From the looks of those flowers, I'd say a woman lives here. She may live alone."

While she and Sammy walked toward the house, Louisa looked at the imaginative designs created in the rock path that led to the door. Someone had worked for weeks or months to haul the stones and lay them out in intricate patterns. Louisa heard a dog barking in response to Sammy's knock. In a few moments, a woman opened the door.

"Come in," she said. She held a white dog to her chest. When the dog yelped, she rubbed its coat and said, "It's okay, Teency. Stop barking."

Immediately, Louisa noticed a special glow radiating from the woman's face. Rays of love seemed to welcome them into her humble home. "Y'all have a seat," the woman said.

Sammy and Louisa walked into the sparsely furnished living room. "Sit right here," the woman said, indicating two straight back chairs. "I'll use this stool." Before she sat down, the woman put the dog on an oval rag rug that covered the center of the floor, and then she reached out to shake hands with Sammy. "I'm Grace Langley. Most people call me Gracie."

"I'm Sammy Grant and this is my wife, Louisa. We're looking for Sandy Hill. Could you tell us how to get there?"

"Sure. Drive south four miles." Gracie pointed that direction. "You'll come to a small community. That's about all there is down there, except a store and school for the kids. Got kinfolks there?"

"No, the District Superintendent of the church wants me to do mission work there," Sammy replied. He reached to pick up Teency and rubbed her coat. "I'll be visiting people to see if we can start church services."

"Wouldn't that be wonderful?" Grace said. Her smile reflected genuine gratitude. "You like Teency? She's got a brother named Tuffy. He's solid black. He belongs to my husband, Luther.

"Would y'all care for a drink of cold water? It's hot today."

"If it's not too much trouble, a drink would taste good," Louisa answered.

"I just drew a bucket while ago. I'll go get you a drink," Grace said. She rose from the stool to walk into another room. She had been gone just a few seconds when a loud noise came from another part of the house. To Louisa, it sounded like a heavy object hitting the floor.

Grace returned to hand them the glasses of water. A look of apprehension replaced the kind smile on her face. "Hurry. Come outside to drink the water. Then you'll have to leave. My husband's been on a drinking binge. Must have bought some moonshine. He just woke up. I'm sorry, but when he's drunk, there's no pleasing him. Come on outside." She ushered Sammy and Louisa out the front door.

"That's too bad," Louisa said, touching Grace on the shoulder. "We'll get out of the your way so things won't get worse." She drank the water and handed the glass to Gracie.

"You say go on south about four miles?" Sammy asked, after emptying his glass.

"That's right," Gracie said, glancing over her shoulder, as if hoping her husband wouldn't step outside. "If you start a church, let me know. Come back for a visit another time." She began walking toward the car as if trying to hasten her guests on their way.

Taking the cue, Sammy and Louisa scooted inside the car and Sammy drove off as fast as possible. Looking backward, Louisa saw a man stumble outside just as Sammy got the car back on the trail. "We made it! I hope that man doesn't take his revenge out on Gracie. She seems to be a sweet person," Louisa commented. "More talkative than an Indian woman would have been."

"Gracie might be the first white woman you can help in this new field," Sammy said.

"And her husband—Luther? —should be the first man you help," Louisa added.

"You would say that," Sammy said, lightly pinching Louisa's cheek.

About twenty minutes later, Sammy and Louisa began noticing signs of life in the area. The trail widened into a two-lane road as they entered a community. Chickens, pecking at sprigs of grass growing between ruts, flew out of the way and squawked as the Grants drove into town. Dogs ran out, baring their teeth and barking loudly.

"The welcoming committee," Sammy commented, smiling at Louisa.

She pointed to the clothes spread on bushes to dry. "It must be washday," she commented. Most of the dwellings were constructed in the board-and-batten style: large flat boards nailed to the wall, and the openings between covered with narrow strips of wood. Flowers and shrubs adorned a few of the yards. Some lawns were framed with wooden fences like Gracie's. Other houses were in various states of disrepair with sagging porches and steps. Dingy tents dotted the landscape, too. Louisa observed a wide range of construction techniques and lawn care.

Like everywhere.

The scene most captivating to her was that of children running back and forth across the road chasing one another. Some were pushing hoops with flat strips of wood. Two girls were swinging a rope while a line of children took turns running in and jumping once or twice before dashing out.

Louisa's heart bounced a bit faster at the sight of the children. Perhaps there'd be a chance to interact with them. Where were the older girls and boys—the ones around Maria's age? If several older students lived in the community, Maria might consider moving to Sandy Hill.

"What do you think, Sammy? Think you can teach Bible stories to these children?"

Sammy leaned toward Louisa to take a closer look at the children frolicking about. He pointed toward a group of boys who seemed to be shooting marbles. Intent on gazing at the children, he didn't raise his foot from the foot pedal. Louisa glanced ahead to see the car heading toward a creek bank.

"Stop, Sam, stop," she yelled, but she was too late. The car sailed toward the stream. Louisa put her head between her knees. By the time Sammy turned his attention to his driving, he couldn't stop before the car nose-dived toward the edge of the creek. Wham! The vehicle came to a bone-jarring stop.

"We're here, but what a way to make an appearance!" Sammy announced. He dropped his head onto the steering wheel while he collected his wits. "We must be at Sandy Hill, but I just didn't see the creek." He raised his head to look at Louisa.

"No, it's not Sandy Hill, it's The Jumping-Off Place," Louisa declared. "You tried to jump that creek, but you didn't make it. Are you hurt? Is the car ruined?" She wriggled around trying to untangle her arms and legs.

"Don't know." Cautiously, Sam tried to unfasten the door on his side of the car. With a little prodding, he was able to open it. He stepped out of the car and walked to Louisa's side. "Try to get out. See if you're hurt," he said, concern covering his face.

Louisa put one foot out of the car and touched the ground. She followed with the other foot and stood up. She felt her arms and legs for injuries. She was relieved to find no visible injuries. By now, the children came running to see about the strangers who had blasted into their community.

"You hurt?" asked an older girl.

"Just my pride," answered Sammy, sheepishly covering his face with his palms. "This is so embarrassing—landing at the edge of the creek on my first trip to a new church." His attempt at laughter caused a flow of blood to rush to Louisa's face.

"Sam, it's not your fault," she protested. "You didn't know there was a bend in the road."

"I should have been watching." He looked at the girl. "I think we're okay, but I wonder about the car—how to get it out of the creek." He walked to the front of the car to look for damage.

Louisa noticed the front tires hanging over the edge of the bank, ready to plunge into the water.

The Lord was watching over us, even if we weren't.

"We've got to get the car away from the bank," Sammy told Louisa.

"I think I know how to do that," a tall, older youth said. "I'll go to the house and get my lariat. I know how to get it out." The boy left in a trot.

"Pull the car out with a rope?" Louisa asked, in a high-pitched voice.

"He's smart," said the older girl. "He's good at figuring things out."

"That's good," Sammy said. "We need a smart person to get us out of the creek. Or we need a lot of strong people to push it out." He paced back and forth behind the car waiting for the young man to bring his rope. "This reminds me of the days when Doc and I went out to treat his patients. We drove over some dangerous bridges, but we always made it."

"Don't worry. There'll be a way to get the front wheels back on solid ground," Louisa said. She turned to the older girl. "Is there a school around here?"

"Yes, Ma'am, during school term. But school's out now."

"How many teachers do you have?"

"Two. One teacher for the big room and one for the little room."

Soon the older youth appeared twirling his lariat.

"How do you plan to pull the car out with the rope?" Sammy asked.

"Cinch it out. Like you tighten a saddle onto a horse," the boy replied. "I'll tie one end of the rope onto the bumper and wrap the other end around that tree trunk. Everybody will pull and then cinch the rope tighter to the tree while we rest. Then we'll pull again, cinch again, till you can back it out. Understand?"

"I certainly do. You fasten the rope to the bumper, then tell the older kids when and how to pull," Sammy said. "I'll tighten the rope around the tree trunk."

This may work, Louisa thought. *It must work.*

Soon, the tires stood on solid ground. Sammy reached out to shake the hand of the youth who had supplied the lariat. "Thanks, young man. You did an excellent job."

The youth shook Sammy's hand. Then, he stared at his worn shoes and replied, "It was nothing. Anybody could have thought of that."

"What's your name?" Louisa asked.

"Maurice Trout," the boy responded. "I go by Marty."

"Nice to meet you, Marty," Sammy said. "You made a good impression. I'm trying to start a church in the community. Do you go to church?"

"Nobody around here goes to church," Marty answered. "We do okay without one."

Uh oh, not a good sign.

"Then our job is cut out for us. Maybe you'll change your mind," Sammy said. He shook Marty's hand again and added, "Thanks for getting the front wheels off the bank." Waving good-by to the children, he nodded to Louisa and they climbed into the car. "Doesn't look good," he mumbled under his breath.

Sammy drove the car around a few curves and parked it near the store where several older men sat on wooden boxes whittling and chewing tobacco while they talked. He climbed from the car and walked toward them. Louisa leaned near the open window to hear the conversation. She watched the men look up at Sammy as he approached them. They gazed at him from head to toe, as if sizing him up.

"Good day, gentlemen," Sammy said, "I'm Samuel Grant, the new preacher in this area. I was wondering if any of you knew where I'll be living."

"A preacher, you say?" asked a man. He spit a chew of tobacco juice about as far as a frog can leap in one try. "You probably got the wrong place. We don't have no church or no preacher. Maybe you should 'a turned left back up the road."

"And you are?" Sammy asked, reaching out to shake his hand.

"Randolph Trout. Go by Randy," he said, shaking Sammy's hand.

"Any kin to Marty Trout?" Sammy asked.

"Yeah, my good-for-nothing grandson. Got plenty of head knowledge, but no horse sense."

"Okay. And you are?" Sammy asked the next man.

"Charles Folsom," came the reply. "I go by Charlie."

"And you, sir?" Sammy asked the last man.

"I'm Warren Kincheloe," the man answered. "Call me Kinny."

"I believe I have this right." Nodding toward each man, Sammy said, "Randy, Charlie, and Kinny. Glad to meet you. I hope I'll be seeing all of you at church services when we get started."

"Not me," said Charlie.

"Nor me, neither," added Kinny.

"Maybe at my funeral," scoffed Randy. "There ain't no preacher's house in Sandy Hill, neither. No use to be looking for one."

Where will we live? Louisa wondered.

"Okay. Thanks, anyway," Sammy said and headed toward the car. He eased into the seat and started the motor.

"We'll drive around and look things over, but I don't think we'll be moving tomorrow like we planned," Sammy said, then sighed deeply. "There's no place to move into, for one thing."

"What'll we do?"

"Go back to Mama's and pray about a making a decision. I wonder if the District Superintendent was aware of the lack of interest in church when he sent us here?"

"Maybe that's why he sent you here," Louisa said thoughtfully.

"Let's knock on a few doors and see if we can get the women together to discuss the possibility of starting a church."

"Set up a meeting when and where?" Louisa asked, rubbing her forehead while she tried to think of a place to talk with a group of women. In a moment she suggested, "How about Thursday at two under the trees at The Jumping-Off Place?"

Sammy laughed in spite of himself. "Fine. Let's stop at a house or two right now."

When they stopped at the next few houses, Louisa noticed the older girl they had met at the creek following them. Louisa called the girl over. "Tell me your name," she said.

"Nadine Trout," the girl answered.

"Oh, are you kin to Marty?"

"He's my big brother."

"Really?" Louisa said. She glanced around for Sammy. "Come here, Sam. The girl who helped us is Marty's sister. Isn't that interesting?"

Sammy hurried over to talk with Nadine. After a while he asked, "Could we get you to help us invite all the women to meet us Thursday at two over at the spot where we nearly ran into the creek?" He pointed toward The Jumping-Off Place.

"I'll see if Pa will let me. He don't have much use for church," Nadine answered.

"And neither does Marty," Louisa said. "I hope that will change. Invite as many women as you can to meet us Thursday, will you? Tell them we're thinking about starting a church."

The girl nodded. Sammy and Louisa got into the car to leave. "We didn't make any progress today," Sammy said as they rode along. "Wonder if Luther is sober yet?"

Chapter Eight

$\mathcal{M}$aria awoke from her nap before Flodell did. Tiptoeing out of the room, she walked through the kitchen and onto the porch. Granny sat in the porch swing doing handiwork. Maria stood for a moment watching Granny pull a threaded needle through a piece of white cloth. "What you doing?" she asked, picking up a corner of the white cloth to inspect it.

"Embroidering a dresser scarf. I noticed you girls were taking naps when I got back from the women's meeting. Is Flodell still asleep?"

"Yes. She needs to sleep because she cries a lot at night; at least she does when I'm in bed with her."

"That girl has some serious problems," Granny said. She clipped the strands with the scissors, and started threading the needle with a length of red thread. "I saw Austin when I was walking back from church. He was riding with the sheriff in his car."

I think I'll ask Granny about Austin's mama.

"Granny, you knew Austin's mama, didn't you? Her name was Lucy Lincoln."

Maria watched a frown cover Granny's face. "That woman was really mean when Caleb was holding your grandpa hostage in the smokehouse," Granny said. "She said all kind of ugly things about his clubfeet . . . like clubfeet causes a person to be dumb. Caleb had a good heart, but being different caused him to get mad at people."

"We were living in Durant then, but Mama told me about Caleb going on a rampage. People like Lucy Lincoln didn't help, did they?"

"Lucy just egged it on."

"At least everything worked out for Caleb to be able to walk now; even if he does use a walking stick," Maria said. "Austin said his mother went off to Hollywood to do dance routines like the Charleston, maybe even be a star in the movies. You think that happened?"

"She didn't deserve it, if she did succeed," Granny said, loudly. "She put that boy of hers on a bus and sent him to boarding school, then took off. That was downright heartless.

"And that sheriff, Lucky Lincoln, didn't even pretend to take care of him. Gave custody over to Brother Solomon. Said he was too busy being sheriff."

"What about his pa? Why didn't Lucy leave Austin with his pa?"

How's Granny gonna answer that?

Granny's back straightened and pulled the needle with a jerk. "Don't reckon he knows who his pa is. He's a Indian, we know that.

"You listen to me, Maria. There's too much of that going on. If we love somebody, we need to get married so the babies will have two parents. Pay attention to your granny."

Maria felt her face growing warm with embarrassment. Why was Granny preaching to her?

"I agree with Granny," said a voice behind her. Turning around, Maria saw Flodell standing in the doorway. "A baby needs two parents living at home. Not one of them off gallivanting around footloose and fancy free, like a certain man named Eli is doing."

"Come sit down beside me, Sis," Granny said, scooting over to make more room. "You don't need to get upset over that man."

Flodell walked to the porch swing and sat beside Granny. She wiped the tears from her cheeks and tried to smile. "I feel better after I took a nap," she said.

"That's good," Granny said.

The three ladies sat quietly, each one lost in her thoughts. Maria wondered if she'd ever find out about whose initials were carved into the tree near Flodell's house. Her thoughts wandered to her parents. Had they found a place to live? Would they be moving the furniture tomorrow? Could she slip off in Brother Solomon's car without her parents' knowledge?

Later in the afternoon, Maria watched Papa's car stop in front of Granny's gate. *Back so soon?* She noticed weariness etched on the faces of both her parents when they got out of the car and walked to the porch. Something bad must have happened.

"What's wrong?" Maria asked, walking toward them.

"There's no place to live," Sammy said, frowning. "We just came by to tell you we won't be moving tomorrow. We have lots of problems to deal with. I guess Granny won't mind you staying with her for a few more days, will she?"

What's going on?

"Maybe not. I'll go ask her," Maria said, stepping inside the house.

In a few minutes, Granny followed Maria out on the porch. "Maria can stay as long as she wants to," Granny said.

"Thanks, Mama," Louisa said.

The group chatted for a few moments. Louisa took Sam by the arm and said, "Let's go. I'm tired."

"Granny, we've got a lot to talk about, but we're both worn out," Sammy said. "We'll come back to talk after we decide what to do with our furniture."

"Furniture?" yelled Maria. "What are you talking about?" She turned to Granny and Flodell. "I'll ride to White Rabbit's with them. I want to know what's going on."

On the way out of town, Maria glanced at the drugstore as they drove by. Was it just this morning that she and Flodell were sitting inside the building, planning their lives? While Maria daydreamed, Louisa went through a quick outline of the happenings at Sandy Hill.

"We'll tell everybody the whole story later," she said.

"Okay," Maria said in a wistful tone. *Will this change my plans?*

Later, while they sat drinking coffee, Sammy launched into detailing the problems he faced. "Papa, the District Superintendent told me to move to Sandy Hill to start mission work. I knew there was no church, but he didn't tell me there was no place to live. I gave up the apartment at Durant—all our furniture is on the trailer—and we have nowhere to live. You're an experienced preacher. Give me your best advice."

Tobias smiled and shook his head. He reached over to pick up his Bible from a table beside the chair. Opening the well worn book, he said, "The best advice is found in Proverbs 3:4-5:

"Trust in the LORD with all thine heart; and lean not unto thine own understanding,

"In all thy ways acknowledge him, and he shall direct thy paths.

"That's what I've always done when I came to a stumbling block in the road. Just trusted . . . "

"I know, I know," Sammy said, squirming in the chair. "But *how* do I do that when I'm out in a canoe without a paddle?"

"For right now, first things first. Let's go hitch the trailer to your car and back it under the barn. You can leave your furniture there so it'll be safe, in case it rains." He placed his Bible on the table and arose from his chair. Maria watched Sammy and Tobias go outside.

"So," Louisa continued, wearily, "you might say we're at the jumping-off place. We've already started calling Sandy Hill 'The Jumping-Off Place'. There's nothing at all in the community to do with a church. The people we talked to don't see the need to have church services."

"That's what you've spent the last few years doing—preparing for this time in your lives," White Rabbit said. "Going to college and getting a education will help, but the most important thing is your trust in the Lord. Like those verses Papa read."

After a while, the backdoor slammed when Tobias and Sammy walked back into the kitchen. They came into the front room and flopped down in chairs. Maria looked at the faces of the dejected group—Mama and Papa with no place to go—White Rabbit and

Tobias wanting to shine a light on the path of their grown children, but not knowing how.

Maybe they won't pay any mind to me being out of the picture.

After a while Sammy spoke to Maria. "Do you want to stay all night with Granny Wade? If you do, I'll take you to town before dark."

"Yeah. I'd better go." She looked into the faces of her mama and grandparents. When would she see them again? She was sneaking off to Durant tomorrow to hide out in a closet in Community Church.

All because I'm in love with a boy, but does Orville love me?

Chapter Nine

As they lay in bed that night, Maria and Flodell discussed their futures. "What are you gonna do?" Maria asked.

"Who knows? I can't stay cramped up in a closet all day while you go to school. Going to Durant with you won't work for me."

"I wish I had a room somewhere. I'd share it with you," Maria said.

"The boy ain't worth it," Flodell said. "You'd better listen to me. I've had experience with a no-good man."

"I told you there was no boy involved," Maria lied.

"But I can read between the lines. Why else would you be so desperate to stay in Durant? You want to be around some boy."

"Oh, hush up. Go to sleep," Maria said, turning her back to Flodell.

Is it as plain as day?

Early the next morning, Maria, Austin, and Caleb loaded into Brother Solomon's car for the trip to Green Briar. Maria told Granny she'd be staying with a friend.

Granny nodded and smiled. She seemed to have no trouble swallowing the lie, Maria thought.

"What are you doing, getting into the car?" Watema asked. "Your parents are moving to a new church."

"No they're not. There's no church, not even a house to live in.

I'm going back to stay with a friend while Papa get things straightened out." *Another lie.*

When the car neared the turnoff to Sandy Hill, Austin pointed toward the road. "Brother Solomon, could we drive up this road a couple of miles? There's something I want you to look at."

"What you think, Watema? Do we have time?" He glanced at Watema waiting for an answer.

"I guess. It seems important to Austin."

Austin directed Brother Solomon to park near the grove of trees. Everyone got out except for Caleb and Watema. "I might fall, trying to walk on the rough ground," Caleb explained.

Maria led the way to the tree with the hearts and initials carved on it. "Do you know whose initials these can be?" she asked. She touched the heart with L. D. L. loves L. A. L. inside it.

"Not right off," Brother Solomon said. He reached in his shirt pocket to get a pencil. "I'll write them down and think on it." He wrote down the letters and folded the paper. Then they were on their way back to the boarding school.

"Why are you so interested in those initials, Austin?" Watema asked.

"I have a feeling that L. A. L are Mama's initials and if they are, maybe the L. D. L. could be my pa's," Austin answered.

"Someone around Riverview ought to know," Watema mused. "Though it may not be revealed for twenty years down the road." She touched Brother Solomon's arm and he smiled at her.

Maria noticed Caleb fidgeting.

There's something going on between them.

"That's a long time to wait," Austin said.

Why not tell Brother Solomon about Flodell's situation?

"Brother Solomon, why don't you and Watema think about helping Flodell Estep with her problems?"

"What problems?" Watema asked. "We don't know Flodell, do we, Frank?"

"No, we don't," he said, turning just enough to see Maria. "Tell us about her problems."

"When we were on our way down here—uh—we happened to pass her house. It was that house out close to the grove of trees where we stopped. Me and Austin were present when her pa kicked her out of the house. She don't have anywhere to live, except with Granny Wade. She needs a roof over her head."

"Her pa treated her like dirt," Austin added.

"There's more to this than what you're telling us," Brother Solomon said. "I know a lot about young people of all ages. Tell me the full story."

"I can't; not in front of everybody."

The air was charged with electricity as if everyone was waiting for an explosion. Except for Brother Solomon, everyone stared at her, waiting for a big announcement. "Why are you looking at me? I can't tell it before you men."

"If that's what you want; so be it," Brother Solomon said.

When the car drove into town, Maria asked to be let off at the bus station. Brother Solomon seemed to hesitate. "Are you sure your parents are aware that you're going back to Durant?"

"Sure. They've got too many problems to work out to worry about me," Maria said, getting out of the car. *Another lie.* "Can Watema get out for a few minutes?"

Brother Solomon nodded in agreement. Maria and Watema walked over to sit on a bench at the bus station. Hurriedly, Maria explained Flodell's problems. "I don't guess she could go to school at Green Briar in her condition, could she?"

"I'll talk it over with Frank. Actually, I'm more worried about you than I am about Flodell," Watema said. "I don't think you're telling the whole truth." She touched Maria's arm and looked into her eyes.

Maria felt herself wilting under the scrutiny.

"If you change your mind, let us know. I hate to see you go on to Durant by yourself."

"Don't worry." Maria stood to go to buy her ticket to Durant. "I'll be back one of these days."

An hour later, Maria stepped off the bus in Durant. She struggled with the idea of whether or not to walk by Orville's house; maybe he'd be out in the yard. She wanted him to know she was back in town. Like a sleepwalker, she headed toward his house on South Seventh Street, two blocks over from Fifth Avenue where she lived—or used to live. Nearing his house, Marie slowed her pace so she'd have plenty of time to scan the front yard and the porch, looking for Orville.

Gall crept up her esophagus when she failed to see her sweetie. With each step, the taste of bile moved up her gullet. By the time she passed Orville's house, the bitterness had reached her throat and was about to burst out in heartrending sobs. But she held back the cries and the tears until she slipped into the alley leading to Fifth.

For a few moments, she stood crying her heart out. Did Orville care whether she had come back to be near him or not? Wait! He could be at her apartment, watching for her return. Maria straightened her shoulders and marched through the alley on to Fifth. Her former home was in view, and someone sat on the steps. He hadn't forgotten her! He was waiting for her! She ran the last few steps, but before she turned onto the sidewalk she realized the boy wasn't Orville. Perhaps the apartment had already been rented.

Wearily, she turned around walked away from Fifth Avenue where college students lived in apartments and houses. Since Maria had lived in this part of town all her life, she knew about all the alleyways and streets. She walked down town, crossed Main Street, and continued a few blocks on to Community Church.

Thankfully, the sun was about to sink. Maria walked more slowly wanting to slip inside the church after dark. She timed her arrival just right and hurried to the back of the church. She turned the knob and the door opened easily. Slipping in quickly, she darted inside the church and closed the door quietly. The church was so dark she had to hold onto the walls to get down the hall. She felt for the door to the closet where she had stored two changes of clothing. Groping in the dark, she touched what she supposed was an oily dust cloth, then she felt a rag mop. Her outfits were inside a bag hidden behind a speaker's lectern out of sight of the janitor. She patted the floor trying to feel her bag of clothes. Her heart jumped to her throat as she wildly grabbed rags, overturned bottles of furniture polish and knocked over mop handles, but she couldn't find any dresses with ruffles on the sleeves and hem.

Why didn't I bring a flashlight?

Maria didn't dare turn on the lights. If a church member saw the lights go on and off, he might come to investigate. After several frantic moments of searching, feeling, and touching everything imaginable, she conceded that her clothes were missing.

Alone in a college town with nothing but the clothes on my back and a few dollars in my pocket.

She fell to the floor of the closet and sobbed.

Where's Orville?

After crying until her head was splitting with pain, she gave up and tried to sleep.

* * *

Sammy and Louisa spent hours trying to find a house to rent till the situation at Sandy Hill was worked out. Louisa wiped tears from her eyes every time she thought of her precious daughter alone in a big college town.

"Our furniture is safe in the barn," Sammy said. "I don't suppose we're in a bind about the church at the bend," Sammy said, laughing at his joke.

Why is he joking when things are falling apart? Louisa wondered. She didn't find it all that humorous. "It's not funny, Sam," she said.

"Mama's glad for us to stay with her. Until we're settled, we can drive to The Jumping-Off Place to start the Lord's work."

"It's going to be hard, serving the Lord in a place we aren't even needed or wanted. At least, according to Marty Trout and his grandpa."

"Maybe Nadine will invite the women to the meeting tomorrow and we can get things started. Let's go check on Maria, if she's still there." He drove past Doc's office and turned the corner to go to Granny Wade's.

At Granny's, Sammy and Louisa learned the ugly truth. A few hours earlier, Maria had left in the car with Brother Solomon. Louisa tried hard, but she couldn't hold back the tears.

"Where did she go? What did she tell you?"

"She said she was going to stay with a friend," Granny responded.

Oh no, she did it!

Louisa burst into tears. "Mama, she told you a lie and you believed it! We already knew she was leaving," she said, between sobs. "We just came by to see if she followed through with her threats. We've got to pray that the Lord takes care of her."

"Why don't you go lie down in your old room, till you calm down?" Sammy asked. "No use crying over spilled milk."

"Yeah, but it still hurts," Louisa sobbed. She sank down onto Granny's porch swing. "I'll rest here for a minute, then we need to take off to Durant. If we have to, you can drag her back by the hair of her head."

"I can?" Sammy asked in a shrill voice. "You'd get mad if I did."

"Now, y'all settle down. Every young person has to try his wings at sometime in his life," Granny said, tersely. "Why, ever one of my kids did things they thought they were hiding. Parents have a way of knowing."

"Sammy, as much as I'd like for you to go to Durant and bring Maria back, I think you need to let her learn a lesson. And it may be a hard one."

"Mama!" yelled Louisa. "You're not siding in with Maria, are you?"

"Not really. I just know how young people think they have to prove things. And sometimes leaving home teaches them a lesson real quick."

For the next hour, Granny, Sammy, and Louisa discussed Maria's well being and safety. Louisa finally agreed to let Maria leave the nest for a few days.

Before they left, Sammy asked Flodell if she'd like to ride with them to Sandy Hill tomorrow when they were to meet with the women of the community. Hesitantly, Flodell agreed. "You'll be driving by my folks' house," she confessed. "I guess I can look at it from the road."

*   *   *

Maria awoke to light shining through the crack around the closet door. She tried to stand, but without room to straighten her legs, that was almost impossible. She reached up to open the door and crawled out of the closet. Holding onto the wall, she was able to stand upright.

Why didn't I bring a pillow? And a flashlight? And a clock? Next time, . . .

"There won't be a next time," she whispered to herself. She walked into a classroom to sit down and make plans for the day. One thing for sure, she wasn't going to be hiding in that closet all day. She needed to eat breakfast so she'd have strength to get out and look for a job. She glanced down at her crumpled dress. No one would hire her if she applied for a job wearing this wrinkled outfit.

Can I buy a dress for a little of nothing? Or could I borrow one?

Maria had no idea of the time. She'd have to go Main Street to look at a clock in a public building. She sneaked out the backdoor of the church and slipped behind a shrub. The row of shrubs beside the church would be a perfect hiding place to walk behind going and coming. At least there was one positive among so many negatives in this escapade! When she walked to the front of the church, she felt no reason to hurry or try to hide. People were always walking out there.

I need a notebook to write in. I sure wish I had something ready to send off to a publisher right now. Wonder how much they pay to publish a story?

Maria managed to fill the day with interesting things. She walked to the park to look at the caged monkeys. Mama had taken her to see the monkeys for as long as she could remember.

What is Mama doing now? Do she and Papa know I'm back in Durant?

An unwanted lump jumped into her throat. She swallowed hard. She loved Orville. Choosing between parents and a sweetheart was like deciding between a piece of chocolate cake and vinegar pie. She felt in her pocket for a handkerchief. Had she run off without a hankie? *Next time . . .*

She turned to watch a young mother whose two children who were playing on the swings. The woman was pushing them and the kids squealed with delight when they stretched out their legs to fly higher in the air. The mother looked so content caring for her children. Maria almost drooled with envy when she remembered Mama pushing her in those same swings.

Wonder if Orville wants a big family?

A visit to the park and a stroll over the campus at the college filled several hours for Maria. Soon it would be time to sneak back into the church. As she left the campus at Southeastern, she stopped at the arches where cars entered. Out of the blue, her eyes stared at a plaque embedded among the rocks in the archway. Maria's heart jumped with wonder. Here, in Durant, was a plaque honoring a man from back in her family's hometown: Thomas LeFlore! He and his wife, Susan, lead of the first group of Choctaws over the Trail of Tears back in 1832. She gazed at the words on the plaque.

THOMAS LEFLORE

1832 BY 1929

J. J. LUCAS

Just reading about someone from her neck of the woods made goose bumps pop out on her arms. Thomas LeFlore had been a Choctaw chief long years ago and he had lived in the chief's house near Swink.

Should she stay in Durant or live at home with her parents? Reading the Chief's name caused a wave of homesickness to sweep over her.

During Maria's first week in Durant, she kept occupied going to many places she and Mama visited. But the routine grew old. She'd have to change to a new activity. This morning, Maria walked to Main Street and entered a department store. She hurried to the women's restroom to look into the mirror. What would she do after she washed her face, combed her hair, and pressed her dress with her hands? Maybe go to Charlotte's and ask to borrow a dress? Was that a good idea? Charlotte's pa might tell Sammy that he'd seen her, if Sammy started asking questions.

Better not go there.

What about knocking on Orville's door and asking his mother to lend her a dress? Not a good idea. She pulled the string to turn on the light and looked into the mirror. She was surprised at the image staring back at her. She had changed so much during the last week of sleeping in a closet! Straggly hair, a bruise on her cheek caused by a falling broom handle while she was wildly digging for her clothes in the dark closet that first night, and a wrinkled dress made for a bedraggled appearance. Would an employer hire her? She had to get another dress to wear before she applied for a job. For a fleeting second she considered "borrowing" a dress from the department store. She hadn't stooped that low yet.

Orville's ma? Charlotte? Visit the First Church and ask for a handout?

She washed her face and combed her hair. There was little she could do about the wrinkles in her dress. A rumble in her stomach reminded her she hadn't eaten in a long time. She'd go eat a bite---a tiny bite. She felt in her pocket for her money. Thank goodness it still there.

The walk to town had used most of Maria's energy. She stepped inside The Little Onion Café, near an alley. A row of round cushioned stools sat before the counter. Maria slipped onto a stool and ordered a glass of milk. She needed to make the milk last a long time, so she drank sparingly. Could she continue to live on one meal a day till she found a job? She put her hand on her brow to rest a moment while she thought over her choices.

Borrow a dress? Look for a job? Go to Charlotte's and eat humble pie?

Humble pie was sounding better every moment, when the door to the café opened. A woman and a girl walked in. Maria almost fell off the stool when she saw the girl wearing her dress with ruffled sleeves and ruffles around the hem.

Where did she get my dress? Do I ask her?

The two customers sat on stools near Maria. She could hear their discussion.

"Where'd you find those two pretty dresses, Mama? I just love this one," the girl said, touching the ruffles on the left sleeve.

"I guess somebody was giving them away . . ."

Giving them away, my foot! I was hiding them.

" . . . When I went to clean at the church, I found them in the closet. I asked Brother Elkins about them. He told me to take them, because someone must have thrown them away. I just can't believe a girl would throw away those nice dresses."

She didn't throw them away.

"It was such a wonderful blessing since you're outgrowing all your clothes. I can't afford to buy a new dress for you right now."

Yes, it was a blessing to you and a curse to me. Finders keepers, losers weepers. And I am about to weep.

Maria gulped the last few swallows of milk from her glass. She needed to get out of the café before she confronted the girl and took back her dress.

Drinking the milk revived Maria's tired body and refreshed her spirits. She decided to go back to the church to arrange the closet for more comfortable sleeping. It didn't take long for her to put the brooms, mops, and dust cloths in a neat arrangement. *I think I'll set them outside the closet tonight, for more room to stretch out.*

With the closet rearranged, how would she fill the empty hours? She decided she'd make a circle around the block where Orville lived about once each hour. Surely, he'd be overjoyed to learn that she was back in Durant.

Every so often, she walked by his house. Disappointment flooded her heart each time she passed with no sight of her sweetie. Did he ever walk out into the yard? Once, she saw a woman, probably his ma, out working in a flowerbed. Better give up the idea of borrowing a dress from her. The woman was too large. Her dress would swallow Maria.

In addition to her hourly surveillance of Orville's residence, Maria needed another task to keep her busy until she started to work. She didn't know what to do with her time. Mama always kept her occupied with sweeping, dusting, or ironing. Now, she had none of that to do.

Perhaps another church needed a janitor? Yes, she knew how to do those tasks. She'd visit at least one church today. Or, if she could find that woman who took her clothes, maybe she could push her in the right direction to find janitorial work. Quickly, she walked to The Little Onion Café to see if the girl who was wearing her dress had returned. Maria stepped into the café. Hurriedly glancing around, she stepped out. The woman wasn't there. She added visits to the café as a part of her routine.

Check Orville's—then go to the café.

But time dragged by. How did she fill the long hours each day until she found a job? What had she always dreamed of doing—back in the days when she lived in the apartment—that didn't cost money? She could go to the picture show—that cost precious money. She was tempted to tell the girl in the ticket booth that she wasn't old enough for a full price ticket, and get a cut rate, but she wondered, *Have I sunk that low?*

When she did go to a picture show, though, she'd try to take a nap while sitting in a cushioned chair. *I could go to the movies at night and get at least two hours of sleep.*

Check Orville's house, go to the show, watch animals in cages and the people at the park, walk over the campus at the college, and buy a glass of milk.

Not much of a daily routine. Right now, she'd go to the First Church to see if they needed a janitor. Maria felt so worthless, walking to the church. Her papa was a preacher, for heaven's sake, and his daughter was about to apply for a position as a janitor. Was she ready for that? Was she hungry enough to sweep and dust the church?

Unless I eat, I won't be able to push a broom.

When she arrived at the church, she saw several cars parked in front. Was a funeral in progress? She was so desperate, she decided to slip in the backdoor to find out what was going on. Stepping inside, she was almost overwhelmed with the scrumptious aroma of food. Were they serving a meal today?

A woman, wearing a checkered bib apron, stepped into the hall. "Are you eating with us?" she asked.

In spite of herself, Maria nodded.

"Follow me. We're just getting ready to serve the meal." The woman smiled at Maria.

Maria stepped into line behind a tall dignified looking man. He was wearing a dark suit. Maria couldn't see the front of his suit, but she assumed he wore a white shirt and tie, too. He was dressed like the preachers she had met at different churches her family had attended. *How low have I dropped?*

She was so hungry that her thoughts didn't dwell on her fall from that social order. She couldn't wait to taste the chicken and dumplings. At long last, she held out her plate for the women to fill it with food. She noticed some women raised their eyebrows when they looked at her. Was she such an outcast that her appearance drew attention to herself? She must replenish her energy supply, though. The disdainful looks didn't bother her like they would have a couple of weeks ago.

Maria found a table where no one else sat. She tried to eat leisurely, but she was so hungry that she found herself wolfing down the food. She had just taken a big bite of chicken and dumplings when a neatly dressed woman sat down beside her. Shaking out her napkin, the lady carefully placed it over the center of her silky navy blue dress.

I forgot to use my napkin, Maria thought. Trying to act nonchalantly, she spread her napkin out like the woman had done.

The woman leaned toward her. "Are you one of Mr. Prescott's close relatives?" she asked.

Swallowing a bite, Maria shook her head. "No. I'm a guest." She wanted to ask about what was the occasion for this lunch, but she was too scared. Noticing a woman seated at another table who wiped tears from eyes, Maria guessed she was at a meal for relatives who had been to the funeral of a loved one. *What have I done now?*

"Are you his housekeeper's daughter?"

"No. Just a guest." *Uninvited.*

"How are you associated with the Prescott Company?" the woman persisted.

"I don't know Mr. Prescott. I came to apply for a job as a janitor, and somehow got invited to eat," Maria confessed. "This is a blessing to me. I haven't had much to eat lately."

"Excuse me for asking, but did how you get that bruise on your cheek?" The woman touched her own face.

Please help, Dear God.

"To be honest, a mop fell and the handle hit me in the face," Maria admitted.

"So you do know how to clean?"

"I learned to walk holding onto a broom—well, almost," Maria answered. "Mama taught me how to do housework since I was real young."

"Your mother was a janitor?"

"No, just a neat housewife." Maria wanted to scream, "*My Papa is a preacher and my folks are respectable people. And I'm not living up to their standards. They would faint if they saw me now.*" But she kept her mouth shut.

The woman patted Maria's arm. "Welcome to First Church," she said. "Eat to your heart's content."

"Thanks."

In spite of the welcome, Maria finished her meal quicker than she had planned. If more folks ask her about her relationship to Mr.

Prescott, she wouldn't know how to answer. She'd spilled the beans about her hunger, already. Wiping her mouth with the napkin, she asked to be excused from the table and slipped out of the dining area.

She stopped in the ladies' room long enough to compose herself. She glanced in the mirror. The bruise was turning purple and yellow; so ugly it's a wonder the fancy lady hadn't run from the sight of her.

Suddenly a dreadful thought hit her. The battered girl she had turned into stood at the jumping-off place in life! The vision of herself teetering on the edge of a cliff hit her with the force of a smack from a razor strap. Tears welled in her eyes. Could she right her self before she fell headlong into a bottomless pit?

She ran from the church crying, forgetting to apply for a job as janitor. She must find a solitary place to hide, because a flood of pent up tears demanded release.

Chapter Ten

Louisa, Sam, and Flodell were returning to Sandy Hill to meet with the women of the community. Flodell pointed to Luther's house. "Have you seen Luther lately?" she asked.

"No, but we really like his wife," Louisa said. *Has it been more than two weeks since we stopped there? And we still haven't heard from Maria.* She blinked the tears back.

"When you pass my house, would you drive slow, so I can see if Mama is out in the yard?"

Sammy slowed down the car for Flodell and Louisa to scan the scene for Flodell's mama. No woman appeared to be in sight. Flodell expelled a loud sigh. "I guess I won't see her today."

Louisa felt as if she were going to cry, too. "I know how you feel, Flodell. We don't know where Maria is. She's been gone more than two weeks, but Mama said Maria needs to try her wings, so we're waiting to see if she is able to fly or comes back to the nest.

"Maybe your ma will be outside when we come back," Louisa continued, trying to comfort Flodell. "You'll probably see her before we see our missing daughter." She tried to keep her tears inside so Flodell wouldn't get more distraught.

Today, Louisa hoped for two women to come for Bible Study at The Jumping-Off Place. "How long have you known Lena Jenkins? You seemed to know each other very well," she said to Flodell.

"Most of my life. Her husband does business with my pa," Flodell responded.

"What kind of business is that?" Sammy asked.

I don't believe the man is in business, thought Louisa.

Flodell seemed flustered about the question. She bit her lips and looked at her hands. Then she put on a sugary smile and answered, "Providing refreshments."

"Okay," Sammy answered.

When they entered Sandy Hill, Louisa wanted to warn Sammy to use caution as he drove into the community, but he beat her to the draw. "I'm not going to drive the car into the creek, Sweet Wife," he said. "You watch the children playing. My eyes are on the road."

Sammy kept the car on the road and pulled to a stop at The Jumping-Off Place.

Louisa sighed when she saw two women standing under a tree, waiting for her and Sammy. The couple stepped out of the car and Flodell followed them. "Why, Mrs. Trout, what are you doing here?" Flodell asked in a shocked voice.

"We're supposed to talk about having church," Mrs. Trout answered.

Sammy reached to shake hands with her. "I'm Sammy Grant and this is my wife, Louisa. You already know Flodell?"

Mrs. Trout stared at the ground for a moment. "Most everybody around knows Flodell's family, especially her pa, Boogie," she replied. "He's the most well known person around here. I'm Mildred, but you can call me Millie for short, Brother Grant."

The group of five stood and talked for a while, waiting for more interested women to appear. Louisa kept looking up the curved lane, expecting a few more ladies, but they didn't come.

Sammy reached in the car for his Bible and thumbed through the pages. He found the verse he wanted to read. "'For where two or three are gathered together in my name, there am I in the midst of them.' That's found in Matthew 18:20.

"So you see, ladies, even though there are only five of us, Christ's Presence can be here with us," Sammy explained. "Just because the number is small, we can't let that hinder us from serving God."

Flodell, Lena, and Millie listened as Sammy explained a few verses about meeting regularly and worshiping God through Scripture and song. "Let's try to have three or four from Sandy Hill next Thursday at two. We need to make plans to start a regular worship time with the Lord."

On the return trip, Flodell asked if Sammy could stop the car near the grove of trees. When they got out, she led Sammy and Louisa to the tree on which the heart was carved. "This heart really interested that boy who was here with Maria. He thought that L. A. L. might be his mama's initials."

"Oh, you mean Austin," Louisa said. "His mother was Lucy Ann Lincoln, so it could be her."

Sammy walked around kicking at empty fruit jars.

"When I was living here, I had to pick up those jars and wash them for the next batch Papa brewed," Flodell said. "I guess he don't have nobody to do that job for him."

Refreshment business? Louisa thought.

"We need to be on our way," Sammy said, suddenly. "We'll think about the initials as we drive along."

"You don't need to worry none. Papa is probably asleep," Flodell said.

However, Sammy pushed for a quick departure. When they had traveled up the road a ways, Louisa saw his shoulders droop and his hands loosen from the steering wheel. "What was your hurry to get away?" she asked.

Sammy turned to look toward Flodell for a moment. "Tell Louisa what refreshment business your pa is in."

"He brews moonshine. But it's supposed to be a secret. Don't tell anybody, especially not the sheriff," Flodell replied.

Louisa and Sammy rode along in shocked silence. Louisa marveled that they were befriending the daughter of a moonshine still operator. *Jesus died for her, too.*

After a while, Louisa got up enough courage to ask Flodell a question. "If your pa brews moonshine why would he kick you out because of your problem?"

"Appearances," Flodell answered. "That still is way off in the woods, hid away from most folks. But people see me most every day."

"Have you decided where you're staying till the baby is born?" Louisa asked, more boldly now. She turned to face Flodell.

"No," Flodell answered. Her lower lip began to quiver. "Maria told me about homes for girls like me that were built by churches. But they're in places like Dallas or Tulsa. I can't go that far away."

"That was sweet of Maria," Louisa said. "Wonder what she's doing today?" She touched Sammy's arm. "What's she doing, Papa?"

"There's no telling. I hope she finds some one to welcome her to the dinner table."

"You don't think she's hungry, do you?" Louisa asked, her voice filled with concern.

"She's probably visiting her friends and staying for a meal," Flodell said. "I'll have to do the same thing once I get out on my own."

"I've been interested in building a cabin for girls who are in your situation," Louisa confessed. "I know where one is located, if you wouldn't mind living alone. Course, I never know if a girl is taking refuge there or not.

"Sam, fixing up a cabin might be a good project for the women at Sandy Hill," Louisa said, tugging at Sammy's shirtsleeve.

Sammy shook his head. "No, that's a touchy subject to start our work off with, don't you think?"

"Touchy, but timely," Louisa said, being careful not to glance at Flodell.

"You mean get them involved in helping others and they may see their own needs?" Sammy asked, thoughtfully. "That might work. If someone would supply the land, you and I could go over there to start building a cabin. From the looks of the lumber scattered around, we should be able to find enough scraps. Wife, I believe I like that idea. Let's pray about it for the next few days."

"When can I go see the cabin you were talking about?" Flodell asked.

"Whenever Sammy has time to drive us over. Or we can catch the train. Which one, Sammy?"

"I'll drive you," Sammy said, rubbing his chin. "I'd like to talk to some of my old teachers at the boarding school while y'all go on to the cabin."

"We'll decide on a day at a later time," Louisa said.

After a while, Sammy parked the car at Granny Wade's. Everyone got out to visit with her before Sammy and Louisa went on to White Rabbit's. Most of the conversation centered about Maria's whereabouts. Abruptly, Flodell got up and left the room. Louisa felt tears stinging her eyes and stood to leave.

As they drove home, Louisa realized Sammy was trying to get her mind off Maria, because he talked about the moonshine still and the cabin at Clear Creek.

"Why would a man who operates a still be so cruel to his daughter when she's in a family way?" he asked.

"Why would a preacher disown his daughter when she's in the same position—through no fault of her own?" Louisa asked. She cried the rest of the way home. For herself and for Maria.

Chapter Eleven

*M*aria's hunger pangs had been put to rest, but with each sob, she felt like another chunk broke off her heart. She lay in a closet squirming around trying to find a comfortable position, while Orville and most likely, Eli, slept on soft beds.

Flodell sure knows a lot about men and boys. They're so unfair. I should have listened to her.

A Voice seemed to whisper to her. *Who made you move here?*

Nobody but that no-good Orville, Maria thought.

Lying on the hardwood floor, Maria weighed her options. Eat humble pie and return home . . . plead with a friend, Charlotte perhaps, to share a bed with her . . . ride to Green Briar to attend boarding school there . . . or what? They all sounded better than the hard floor she was lying on. The thoughts of vinegar, simmering on the stove with sugar and spices, brought tears to her eyes. When would she taste another bite of vinegar pie?

The next morning, Maria counted her change. She decided she had enough to buy a glass of milk before she returned to First Church to apply for a job as janitor. She needed the energy, should she begin work today. She walked to The Little Onion Café and slipped to her usual place. By now, the proprietor was aware she always ordered a glass of milk. He set it on the counter before she asked for it.

Not long afterward, the girl who wore her dress came in with her mother. Maria's blue dress had been freshly washed and ironed. Marie looked down at the wrinkled dress she wore. She fumed with anger. *How dare she wear my dress?* She watched as the girl played with her silverware while she and her mother waited for their order.

It must be payday for the church janitor.

Maria was salivating with hunger when she watched the owner slide two pieces of pie heaping with meringue toward them. Even without sniffing, she recognized the aroma —lemon!

I hope the church is serving lunch today. I'm sorry, Dear Lord. I don't want anyone to die. Maybe there's a lunch for some kind of women's meeting.

You don't go to women's meetings, her conscience told her.

Maria was about finished with her milk when the girl spoke, loud enough that Maria heard. "Mama, the preacher's daughter has a new feller."

"Hush. You shouldn't be talking about Charlotte that way," her mother said.

"Well, she told me she was sweet on a boy."

"Don't be repeating that in public. Brother Elkins might get mad and I'd lose my job."

"I just thought you'd want to know that Charlotte is in love with Orville."

Maria's head fell to the table with a thud. Not her Orville. Of course not. There were many more boys living in town named Orville.

"That's enough. Don't mention it again," the girl's mother said, harshly. Maria saw her looking her way. "If the news got out, Brother Elkins might accuse you of gossiping. "

Maria didn't believe the girl. She was fibbing to her mother. Still, she needed to find out for sure. She was staying in Durant because of her love for Orville, for heaven's sake. It would be foolish for her to live in a closet because she loved a boy who cared for another girl. She jumped from the seat so fast, she knocked over her glass, but it was empty. She hurried out of the café. She started toward First Church to try for a job.

By the time she reached the church, she was fuming with frustration. She walked to the back of the church to enter, hoping to smell chicken and dumplings again. She sniffed the aroma of coffee. She hadn't had a taste of coffee since she came to live in Durant, but she probably wouldn't be partaking of it today. She strode down the hall, peeking in doors. Finally, she decided she had found the pastor's office. She lifted her hand to knock, but stopped when she heard a woman speaking.

"Pastor, I met the most pathetic-looking girl yesterday," the voice said.

Surely not me?

"Where was that, Sister Grimes?"

"Here at church . . . "

Maria's felt her face burning with shame. She had fallen into disgrace, but not far enough to endure the term "pathetic." She turned to leave the church. As she hurried down the hall, the woman who, yesterday, wore an apron, stepped out again.

"Did you come to the Ladies' Aid Meeting?" she asked.

"Yeah. I came for aid," she answered, trying to control the bitterness in her tone. "I came for aid yesterday, but you asked me to eat and I did. I came again today to see if you needed a janitor to clean the church, but I know you don't, so I'll leave."

"What's your name?"

"Maria."

"Why don't you come eat some cookies and have a cup of coffee? I'll bet it would help stop your hunger pangs."

Do they have vinegar pie?

"Would it be okay?" Maria asked, weakening.

"Sure, come on in," the woman urged. She took Maria's arm and ushered her into dining area. "The women aren't here yet. Take a plate and get all the desserts you want."

"You don't have any vinegar pie, do you?"

Why did I ask that?

"Why, yes we do. I'll get you some. There's an Indian woman who always brings vinegar pie to church meals."

"Several of my kinfolks really do like it. We're Choctaw."

Maria sat down, trying to eat slowly, but she was too hungry to use good manners. She knew Mama would really fuss if she saw her eating so fast.

"Tell me about yourself," the woman suggested. "I'm Mrs. Barnes. Church folks call me Cleta."

"There's nothing to tell," Maria said. *A lie.* She stuffed her mouth with pie so she wouldn't tell about living in a closet—with no changes of clothes—with no food to eat. Because of a feller who was fickle. Before she had time to think, Maria blurted out, "Are you married?"

"Oh, my yes. I've been married for twenty-five years. Why did you ask?"

"I was thinking about getting married. Are your children married?"

"Yes. I have five grown married children and two grandchildren," Cleta answered. She smiled.

Maria broke a piece of flaky pie crust with her fork. "I don't even know how to make pie crust," she ventured. "I help Mama sweep, and dust and mop, but I never was interested in cooking. I guess I need to learn to cook before I get married. What do you think?"

"When you first get married, if your husband is head over heels in love, he won't worry about the food," Cleta replied. "After a while, he starts to notice if the biscuits are done and if the other foods are ready to serve."

"What do the Ladies' Aid women do?" Maria asked.

"They help people in need—like sewing baby clothes, helping children in the orphans' homes. They just help anybody in need."

I'm in the right place.

"Are there any jobs the Ladies' Aid women need done, for a donation? I need a job real bad."

"Why don't you come back in an hour and you can ask the women yourself?"

"Thank you. I really did like the coffee and desserts, especially my favorite, vinegar pie," Maria said, feeling about important as Tuffy, when he was in the back of Eli's car.

Tuffy! I was scared back then, but I was happy. Austin was good to me.

Maria left the church planning to return in an hour. She decided to go back to Brother Elkin's church to rest a while. Maybe she could lay her head on a table and take a nap. Usually no one came into the church during the day except on Sundays. She had just stepped into a classroom to rest, when she heard the backdoor slam. Her heart jumped into her throat and she dashed toward the closet. She closed the closet door silently, just as she heard a young woman's voice—Charlotte's? She turned, pressing her back against the wall. No need for her feet to be showing in the crack at the bottom of the door. When the people neared the closet, Maria heard two sets of feet walking down the hall. A young man spoke. Maria had no doubt that two people were passing by. The male voice sounded too familiar—she knew it belonged to Orville.

"I thought you already had a girlfriend," Charlotte was saying. She giggled.

Sounds silly to me. Like a lovesick calf.

"Who would that be?" Orville asked.

It's me! Tell Charlotte you love me!

"Maria Grant sure likes you."

"Huh. She may like me, but I care nothing for her," Orville said. "She's been going by my house ever day for more than two weeks, and I have to hide ever . . . "

Maria strained but she couldn't hear the rest of Orville's reply. Only the clunking of two pairs of shoes strolling down the hall. She wanted to fall in the floor and bawl, but why? She had heard Orville proclaim that he cared nothing for her. He had even been hiding from her! Now, she needed to wash her hands of Orville and start life over. Where? Certainly not in Durant.

Chapter Twelve

When Maria was positive that Orville and Charlotte had left the church, she opened the closet door to see if she had any possessions left. She wouldn't be sleeping in the storage closet another night. She was leaving—for an unknown destination. She dug through her purse to pull out all the money she had left. Was there enough to ride the bus or train to Riverview or somewhere else? She was heading out of town; that was for sure.

Without a backward glance—not even walking by Orville's house to see if he was outside—she rushed to the depot. She had enough money to buy a train ticket to Piney Ridge. She could walk to Clear Creek Boarding School and stay in the cabin tonight. Then, she'd decide how to get on to Riverview.

Maria trembled as she dug the last pennies from the bottom of her purse to buy the ticket. Her happiness was overshadowed with heartache and weariness. Why did Orville hide from her? Why didn't he just come out on the porch and tell her he didn't care for her?

All this pain, and she would be punished, too. It didn't matter. She'd tell Mama and Papa she was sorry she ran away from home. She would be willing to mop, sweep, and dust for hours at a time when she got rested up.

She felt tears stinging her eyes, but they were tears of exhilaration . . . or was she just so tired she wanted to cry? She knew she'd be content to move to The Jumping-Off Place where Papa was going to start a church.

Boys are so unreliable. I wonder if I'll ever trust one again.

If she'd had the energy, she would have danced up the steps onto the train. The strings to Orville had been broken even though it hurt. She was loosed from Orville! When she sank into her seat on the train, she felt as if outstretched arms were enfolding her. She knew the clattering wheels of the train would lull her to sleep. Sleeping on the floor in the closet had felt like she was lying on a flat rock.

I've got to be careful to wake up or I won't get off at Piney Ridge.

Squirming around, she had found a perfect resting position when a young man sat in the seat beside her.

"I won't bother you," he said, tipping his hat.

"As tired as I am, I doubt you could bother me. I'm gonna take a nap till we get to Piney Ridge."

"I'm studying to preach my first sermon this Sunday at Riverview, so I'll be meditating and thinking. I'll be quiet."

"My grandpa, Tobias Grant, is the preacher at the Indian Church. Is that where you're preaching?"

Has something happened to Tobias?

"Yes."

"Is Tobias sick? I've been away lately."

"No. This is a practice sermon for me. As far as I know your grandpa is okay. I'll be quiet so you can sleep."

"That's okay," Maria replied, sleepily. "My papa's a preacher, too. He preached his first sermon at Riverview several years ago."

"At the Indian Church?"

"Yes. Papa's a twin. From the way my folks tell it, one twin preached and the other one played the organ."

"So you go to church often?"

"Every Sunday, almost that is . . ."

I haven't been going to preaching lately.

"By the way, my name is Jonathan Folsom," the young man said. "What's your name?"

"I'm Maria Grant," she answered. "If I was in Riverview Sunday, I'd come to hear you preach, but Papa has moved to a new church. He's doing mission work at Sandy Hill. I'll—"

"That's where I'm from! I'll be visiting my folks while I'm here. I may meet your parents if we're there at the same time." Jonathan thumbed through his Bible. Opening it, he placed it on his lap.

"I'm going to try to preach on the Prodigal Son."

What about the prodigal daughter?

By now, Maria was fully awake. She reached out a trembling hand to shake Jonathan's hand. "Glad to meet you. I'm the prodigal daughter. Ask me some questions. I may be able to answer them because now I'm returning home." She laughed faintly, but she meant every word.

"But you're so young!" Jonathan protested.

"And so headstrong and pigheaded. Look at me," she said, lightly touching her dirty wrinkled dress, "I just climbed out of the pigpen."

"If you don't mind my asking, what led you to go to the pigpen?"

"I don't mind. I'll tell you and then it may be easier for me to tell my parents. Why did I go to the pigpen?" Maria closed her eyes to think a moment. Pictures of Orville came into her mind. He didn't look as handsome now as before.

"Would you believe it was a boy?"

"Sure. Many events in history have happened because of the love between a man and a woman. Even the lives of kings and queens have been altered because of love. Tell me more."

"When Papa said we were moving to Sandy Hill, in my heart I said, 'No.' I started looking for a family to live with, but I couldn't find one. I wanted to be near a boy I thought I was in love with."

"Where did you end up staying?"

"Look at me," Maria repeated. "Does it look like I've been living in a church?"

Jonathan seemed flustered by the question. "Apparently not."

"But I have! I've been sleeping in a broom closet at a church. The floor was really hard."

"You poor girl. Did the boy know about the awful sleeping conditions?"

"I thought the *boy* never knew I was around, but this very day he said he had been hiding from me. I heard it out of his mouth. He said that he didn't care for me." She paused for a moment to calm her wildly beating heart. "When he said he didn't like me, that was the minute I decided to go back home to my parents. I hope they will accept me."

If the Bible is true, they will.

"But how did you eat? Did you have enough money to buy food?"

Maria laughed, weakly. "I drank a lot of milk. And I did eat at church meals a couple of times. I would gladly have eaten the leftover scraps from somebody's plate any time. I believe I know how it feels to be hungry. There was plenty of food on my granny's table—I just wasn't there to partake of it. I had clean clothes at home to wear, but I had to wear this one dress all the time. I've learned my lesson."

"I need to ask a question. It's only for my sermon," he explained. He put his finger on a verse to read. "The Bible says that the prodigal ' . . . joined himself to a citizen of that country; and he sent him into the fields to feed swine'. I believe that means he associated with some rough characters—you didn't do that, did you?" He fidgeted as if hoping she hadn't.

Maria smiled. She believed Jonathan was embarrassed when he asked the question. "No, I didn't. But who knows? If a rough character had invited me to have a meal with him, I was so desperate, probably I would have done it." She rubbed her eyes and stifled a yawn.

"Thank God for that. Why don't you go ahead and take a nap? I'll wake you up when we get to Piney Ridge."

"Thanks." Maria found the perfect sleeping place and dozed off. It seemed she'd just closed her eyes, when she felt Jonathan's hand gently shaking her.

"Time to get off the train," he said.

When they had walked down the steps, Jonathan led her to a bench at the depot. "I got off with you because I want to offer you something," he said, somewhat hesitantly. "Would you like to go with me to my grandmother's house and get cleaned up so you'll look better when you see your parents? Grandmother may have a dress you can wear."

"But why? You don't know me," Maria protested. In her heart, she yearned for clean clothes and a clean body to put them on.

"Ever heard of the Ladies' Aid Society at church? My grandmother belongs to one and she'd love to help you. She's that kind of woman."

"I met a woman from the Ladies' Aid and I trusted her. I'll trust you. Let's go."

A while later, Maria stepped from Grandmother Folsom's bathroom, clean and dressed in a dirt free outfit. It didn't matter if the outfit was too big, she felt refreshed.

"Thank you very much. I'm not in the pigpen any longer and it feels so good."

Chapter Thirteen

Louisa and Flodell sat under a tree at Green Briar visiting with Watema. The men folks had walked over to look at a batch of new puppies belonging to Austin's dog.

Watema shook her head in mock dismay. "I never dreamed Frank would allow Austin to keep a litter of pups."

"Better pups than some other creatures I know about," Louisa said, glancing toward the men. She made sure no one was with in hearing distance, and then she continued, "We're going to the cabin at Clear Creek to see what it needs. At Sandy Hill, Sammy and I are thinking about getting some folks to build a cabin for girls who want to be out of the public eye for a while."

Flodell pulled at blades of grass while Louisa spoke. "It's embarrassing," she muttered.

"Yes, we know," Watema said. She smiled at Flodell. "But a cabin gives a good hiding place away from nosy women. Did you want to stay at the cabin at Clear Creek?" she asked.

Flodell's face flushed with humiliation. "I wanted to look at it. I brought my clothes, in case I decide to stay. Maria said she told you my pa kicked me out, didn't she?"

Watema nodded.

"I don't have no place to live. Granny Wade is letting me stay with her now, but I need to move somewhere else for a while."

"Even though Maria slipped off and went back to Durant, she showed concern for you, Flodell," Louisa said. She fought back tears. "That was kind of her."

"I imagine she had a feller she couldn't stand to leave," Flodell said.

"No! She couldn't be living in Durant just to be close to a boy," Louisa exclaimed. She raked her fingers through her black hair.

That can't be true.

"Worse things than that have been done before," Watema said.

"You're scaring me," Louisa said, wrapping her arms around her body. "My little girl, willing to stay alone in a college town, just because she thinks she's in love!"

"I accused her of that, but she wouldn't admit it," Flodell admitted.

"There, you see! She didn't leave home to be near a boy," Louisa said.

Please, Lord, don't let it be so.

"Watema, would you like to go with us to the cabin?"

"Sure. I'd like to see the place where me and Caleb stayed. And where we met Austin. I got a lot of memories from that cabin."

"Why don't we take some food and have a picnic? Of course, we never know if another girl is staying there or not," Louisa said, thoughtfully.

Later in the day, two carloads of folks drove onto the grounds at Clear Creek Boarding School. The men unloaded a basket of food and set in on the grass while they took a few minutes to reminisce about their days of living there.

Jim came out and volunteered to drive the wagon to take them to cabin. "I have a suspicion that someone is over there now," he said. "I saw a girl walking that way earlier today."

Louisa felt a ripple of excitement fly through her at the thought of seeing a girl taking advantage of sleeping on the soft bed she had provided at the cabin. "Let's hurry over to meet her." She was so delighted she believed she could outrun the wagon.

Jim stopped the wagon in front of the porch and all the passengers jumped out except for Caleb. Austin and Sammy helped him down. Louisa hurried to knock on the door. "Anyone here?" she called.

Wonder who the new girl is?

*   *   *

Maria awoke to the loud rapping on the door. A shiver of fright ran down her spine. Who could be here and what did they want? She sat up on the side of the cot and slipped her feet into her shoes. Her muscles quivered from weakness as she wobbled to the door to open it. She couldn't believe her eyes. Maybe she was hallucinating. It couldn't be her mama!

"Mama," she whispered. "How—did—you—know—I—was—here?" She began sobbing uncontrollably.

"Maria! What are you doing here?" Louisa exclaimed. "We thought you were in Durant. Come out and explain all this to us."

Maria couldn't stop crying. She was unable to speak. Sammy and Louisa helped to seat her in a chair on the porch, trying to comfort her.

So weak . . . can't even think.

Watema kept her wits about her. She walked over to the picnic basket and pulled out a sandwich for Maria. "When she gets some food in her stomach, she'll feel better," she said.

Maria nodded and took the sandwich from Watema. The aroma told her it was delicious bologna.

"Have you been here all the time?"

"What did you have to eat?"

"Where did you get your dress? It's way too big."

"Were you scared at night?"

Maria shook her head in bewilderment, and then she ate a bite from the sandwich. She couldn't answer all the questions at the same time. The feelings of love shown by her family overwhelmed her. She felt contentment envelope her because of the love surrounding her, but she couldn't speak. These people cared! She had run away from their love. How had she ever sunk to such depths as to cast away the family who really cared for her? The thoughts of her family's care caused her to sob convulsively. She felt unworthy of their concern. She gazed at the frightened faces staring at her in disbelief.

At Mama's tearstained face . . . at the look of grave concern on Papa's face . . . the anxiety in Watema's eyes . . . the pity in Caleb's stare . . . the acceptance in Austin's smile . . . the love in Brother Solomon's gaze. They cared! They cared! Orville cared not a speck. She had sacrificed so much for him, but he had spurned her love. She covered her face with her hands and sobbed till there were no more tears to flow.

The Holy Spirit revealed not only had she spurned the love of her relatives; she had spurned the love shown her by Jesus. She had treated Him the same way she had done her family. She must repent and ask for forgiveness from Him and from her loved ones.

"I'm so tired," she said, weakly, "but I ask forgiveness from y'all and from Jesus. I'm a prodigal daughter who's come home. I didn't care about anybody but my self—and—and—a boy. But I'm too tired to talk now."

Maria tried to stand, but her knees buckled beneath her. She felt Papa's strong arm around her shoulders as he guided her back inside the cabin and laid her on the cot. Mama pulled the cover around her neck and whispered, "Welcome home. Go back to sleep."

*　　*　　*

When Maria awoke, she was lying in her mama's bed back at Granny Wade's house. She tried to sit up on one elbow, but fell onto the bed. "How did I get back here?" she asked. "The last thing I remember I was at the cabin."

"That was yesterday," Louisa said, patting her on the arm. "You must have been tired out because you've slept around the clock. Do you feel better now?"

"Yeah. It's so much different sleeping in this bed than it was sleeping on the floor." She knew the food was different, too. Dare she ask for her favorite food? "Could I have some vinegar pie?"

"Mama thought you'd want some, so she made a pie after we brought you home. You were dead to the world."

Maria pushed at the patchwork quilt and tried to get out of bed, but her legs wouldn't work. *Why am I so tired?*

"Sammy," Louisa called. "Will you come help me carry this girl to the kitchen table? She wants to eat some vinegar pie."

"Mama would you get a saucer of pie for Maria?"

Soon, Maria sat at the table savoring her favorite food. "This is so-o-o good," she said, between bites.

"You need to go slow on the eating. From the looks of your skinny arms and legs, you haven't had much to eat," Granny Wade said.

"All I had was glasses of milk I bought at The Little Onion Café. I ate two times at the First Church. Those ladies were nice to me." Her head fell onto the checkered tablecloth.

"It looks like the owner of The Little Onion would have given you some leftover food," Louisa complained.

"How I wanted something to eat! Nobody knows," Maria said. She felt tears scalding her eyes. She raised her head and took a bite of pie to choke back the sniffles.

"If you were so hungry, what made you decide to come to the cabin?" Sammy asked. "There's no food there."

"I didn't have enough money to buy a ticket to Riverview, so I bought one to Piney Ridge, then a new friend brought me to Clear Creek. I walked on to the cabin to sleep till the next day. Almost had to crawl I was so tired, but I would have found a way to get here. I'm glad y'all came before I had a chance to leave."

"Who's this new friend?" Sammy asked. A look of concern covered his face.

"Don't worry. I'm not in love with him. He's a young preacher," Maria answered.

"It looks to me like you would have learned your lesson—," Sammy began.

Louisa grabbed his arm. "Now wait a minute, Sam. Let her explain," she said. "Just because one young man is a rotten apple doesn't mean the whole barrel's bad."

"Y'all can meet him at church Sunday. He said he was preaching there; that it was like practicing learning how to preach. I hope I feel like going. I helped him with the sermon."

"What?" Sammy hollered. "That sounds fishy to me."

Maria tried to smile. "It's a pig sermon.

"Good pie, Granny. Thank you. Papa, I need to rest some more so I'll be able to go to church Sunday."

"Wonder who this person is, you're wanting to hear preach?" Sammy muttered.

"Don't worry. You'll like him. In a way, he's like you." She walked to the bed to rest.

A while later, Maria awoke feeling more revived. She opened her eyes to see Louisa hovering over the bed, like a mother hen plumping up her nest. "I'm better now, Mama," she whispered. She looked around. She felt cozy in this room with family pictures hanging on the wall and a soft bed. She fluffed the feather pillow and snuggled deep in the feather bed. She'd lie here a while and reminisce.

"It's like Jonathan said. The father of the Prodigal Son never gave up. Everyday, he went out looking for his son to return," Maria whispered to herself.

"I know you were looking for me everyday, too," she said aloud, trancelike.

"What are you talking about?" Mama asked.

"Just thinking out loud, Mama," Maria answered. "I've been like the Prodigal Son. I came back to a family who cares."

"Yes, you did," Mama replied.

Maria lay there coming in and out of wakefulness. Occasionally, the odor of a musty closet wafted in, only to be chased away by a wave of stench from the horrible smell of a pigpen. She compared the Prodigal Son, working in the pigpen and eating husks, with her life penned in a storage closet. The son had left home wanting his own way.

So did I. I imagine the young man had big dreams when he walked away from home. I had big dreams for Orville and me. Me and the prodigal both left home with high hopes.

A tear trickled down the side of her face. Such big dreams! Such big crashes! Maria wondered if she was like the prodigal in every way, because he went on a spending spree. She sure didn't.

He wasted his substance in riotous living, a Voice corrected.

What does riotous mean?

"Mama," she yelled. "Would you do something for me? Bring me a dictionary."

Soon, Louisa came with a huge dictionary: the one her papa had used when he prepared sermons. "What are you wanting to learn about?" she asked.

"The meaning of a word," Maria answered. She had trouble handling the big book—finally placing it on the mattress and searching for the word. She found a whole string of synonyms describing riotous, but the two that best described her behavior were *rebellious* and *uncontrolled.*

Yeah. I was rebellious and uncontrolled. I wasted my life on that kind of living.

It wasn't for long, however, because the prodigal began to be in want and so did she. She wanted bread and meat and desserts. Twice, she ate with strangers at church. These unfamiliar people were kind, though. Most of the time, she and the prodigal could expect no help from any creature.

Maria hoped in his sermon, Jonathan explained the stages the prodigal lived through on his downward path. Jonathan probably didn't even know how to put them into words, because he was so kind.

I doubt he ever had a wayward thought.

She realized that, after they considered themselves as dead and lost, she and the prodigal both came to themselves.

I had clothes and food at home, but there I was, shut up in a closet! I decided to arise and go . . .

An old-time hymn sneaked into her mind. She started humming it—then, she began singing it softly.

> "I will arise and go to Jesus,
> He will embrace me in His arms;
> In the arms of my dear Savior,
> Oh, there are ten thousand charms."

She sang and she sniffled. The song told the story of her life, inside and out. Suddenly, she realized someone was standing over her. Mama and Granny Wade were listening to her song.

"I'm singing a song about the Prodigal Son," Maria explained.

Until now, Maria wasn't aware of the toll this episode had taken on her body. She shuddered to recall the nights of sleeping on a hard floor while she breathed the musty oily scent of the mop and dust cloths. Going without food had weakened her body's defense system. It might take a few days to get over the experience. She'd have to live life a day at a time. She was deeply grateful to be back in a place where she felt love, though not boldly spoken. She must work hard to repay Mama and Papa for the torment she had put them through. How could she show her gratitude to them for their unswerving love?

"I'll find a way," she said. She turned over to fall asleep again.

*   *   *

Later, sitting at the kitchen table with Mama, Papa, and Granny Wade, Maria realized she hadn't seen Flodell lately.

"I haven't seen Flodell since I've been back in Riverview. Did she decide to stay at the cabin?"

"She's at Watema's. She and Caleb are getting acquainted, because Caleb asked her to marry him. And she said yes. Can you believe it?"

Oh, no, I missed the wedding.

"Did they get married while I was away?" Maria asked

Louisa shook her head. "No. When you're up and around, they'll get married. We'll go to the wedding. Mama wants to go with us. A bunch of the family wants to go."

"Caleb must be a good catch, because Flodell knows all about men and boys," Maria admitted. "She accused me of sneaking off to Durant because of a boy, but I wouldn't confess to it."

"Just who was this boy you couldn't stand to be away from?" Sammy asked.

Maria felt her face burning with shame. "Do I have to tell? It's so embarrassing."

Granny Wade squeezed Maria's hand. "Your parents would feel better if they knew," she said.

"Okay. It's that lowdown civet cat, Orville," Maria confessed.

"Not Orville Sutton!" Louisa exclaimed. "I always liked him."

Sammy agreed. "I did, too."

"He cared nothing for me. I heard the words come out of his mouth. After all I went through." Maria heard her voice quavering. *I need to be careful.* She took a deep breath and continued, "It was like a knife stabbing my heart when he said that. Him and Charlotte were walking down the hall at church when he told Charlotte he saw me passing his house and he hid every time. He didn't know I heard him talking cause I was in the closet. That's when I decided to come back home. That very minute, I started getting ready to leave."

"It's a blessing that part of your life is behind you," Louisa said. "There's plenty more fish in the pond. And you've got plenty of time to catch a feller."

"I don't know if I'll ever trust another boy again or not," Maria said. She felt her face heating up with embarrassment from all this talk about trying to catch a feller.

Chapter Fourteen

*C*aleb and Flodell strolled beneath the pines on the campus at Green Briar Boarding School. Caleb walked slowly, because his artificial feet and legs were not easy to maneuver. His ability to move about had improved an enormous amount since the amputations, but not as easily as real feet moved.

"Flodell, I don't expect you to be sweet on me on such short notice," he confessed, dropping onto a bench. He patted the space beside him, inviting Flodell to rest with him. He took her hand and noticed how small it was compared to his. "That day at the cabin, I realized lots of people were there who had practically given their lives for me. Why couldn't I help somebody?"

"Help who?"

"You. I noticed how sad you looked and I couldn't help but put you and Mary together."

"Mary who?" Flodell stared into Caleb's eyes. She seemed puzzled.

"Mary, the mother of Jesus."

"Oh, I see," Flodell said, covering her face. She appeared self-conscious at her ignorance.

"For one thing, I understood that when Joseph took Mary as his wife, he was helping a young girl who was in a embarrassing situation. I knew you felt like you was washed up salt creek."

Am I doing this right? Does she understand?

"Yeah. That pretty well describes it," Flodell said, twisting a strand of hair around her finger. "I felt like I was walking on hot coals when Pa kicked me out of the house. He said not to come back without a marriage license in one hand and holding a man's hand with the other."

"You know I can't get around as fast as most men, because part of my legs and all of my feet are gone. My heart's all there, though." He tapped the spot on his chest where he thought his heart should be.

"Your warm heart will ease my pain. I'll be a good wife. Ever time we go for a walk, I like you that much better."

Caleb hugged Flodell tightly. "Thanks. I feel the same way about you. Just as soon as we hear from Maria, we'll go to the cabin to get married."

*   *   *

Two days later, a few cars parked at Clear Creek Boarding School. Several people, wearing their best clothes, got out of cars. They crowded around Caleb and Flodell, laughing and teasing them. Flodell was radiant, wearing her fancy purple dress with ruffles around the neck, sleeves, and hem. She carried a bouquet of flowers, the center of which was filled with purple petunias. Caleb wore a pure white shirt and black trousers. His blue-black hair had been plaited in a long single braid that lay on his back. Soon, Jim drove up in the wagon for the bride and groom to ride to the cabin. Tobias, Flodell, White Rabbit, Granny Wade, Watema, and Brother Solomon rode in wagon. Everyone else walked, skipped, or ran.

Maria believed she was able to walk to the cabin. She noticed that either Mama or Papa stayed by her side her constantly.

Probably afraid I'll fall, but I made it the other day when I was real weak.

As they walked, Sammy began to sing *Amazing Grace* in Choctaw. Soon, the entire group was singing together; some sang in English, others Choctaw. Maria watched the young kids turning cartwheels.

She and Austin joined hands, swinging them to keep time with the singing. When Maria noticed a dignified young man walking with the group, she pulled away from Austin. Jonathan! She started shaking and her heart jumped to her throat. She didn't want Jonathan to think she and Austin were lovers.

What's Jonathan doing here?

When the last guests reached the cabin and the passengers in the wagon had unloaded, Tobias called out to get everyone's attention. He took Jonathan by the arm and led him to the porch.

"*Halito* (Hello). I want you to make Jonathan Folsom welcome. He's surrendered to the ministry and he'll be preaching at our church Sunday. Today, he's here to observe the marriage ceremony. Someday, he'll be performing weddings.

"Welcome, Jonathan."

Most everyone clapped. Maria noticed Papa looking Jonathan over with an eagle eye.

You can trust him, she thought. She wanted to run to speak to Jonathan, but she knew Indian girls didn't approach older boys when they were out in the open. If they were alone behind the cabin, she'd speak to him, but not where everyone could stare at her. Many signals were given through the way they looked at each other. They could read the gestures and silent hints. Once the ice was broken between family members, much hilarity took place.

Such as today—everyone was laughing and joking. The wedding at the cabin was not a traditional ceremony. There would be no feasting and dancing here, just repeating the vows and tying the matrimonial knot. The location was of significance to Caleb. It was on this porch that Watema told him she was his mother. Brother Solomon had revealed he was Caleb's father. The *marriage* was of major importance to Flodell. To be back in the good graces of public eye, not having to hide out until the birth of the baby were her concerns. Now the cloud of shame would vanish. The feasting and dancing would take place at Brother Solomon's house back at Green Briar.

Brother Solomon had been chosen to perform the wedding. He asked Caleb and Flodell to stand on the porch so everyone could see them. He performed a simple ceremony. The bride and groom promised to love each other until death "do us part."

The weeks of hiding out had taken their toll on Maria's body. She was so weak she couldn't control her emotions, but she didn't try hard. To think that Caleb, who had spent almost twenty-five years of his life as a cripple, was now going to live a nearly normal life—the thought overwhelmed her. And, Flodell, who had been raised practically in the shade of a moonshine still, was going to become a respected housewife—the thoughts were humbling. No wonder Papa sang *Amazing Grace* as he walked along. Grace had brought them safe thus far and grace would lead them home.

God is good. He took me and Flodell out of the pigpens and put us in our own homes.

Maria felt a shadow cast over her. "You're looking better," Jonathan said. "You'll be able to come to church Sunday, I hope?"

She nodded. "I'm planning to come, if this wedding doesn't drain me dry," she said, wiping tears from her eyes. "Just barely existing as a prodigal took a lot out of me." She looked at folks milling around and pointed out her family members "There's my mama and papa, Louisa and Sam Grant. Over there are my grandparents, Tobias and White Rabbit Grant. You already know he's the preacher at Riverview Indian Church. And the woman over there is my other grandmother—Granny Wade." She scanned the crowd for other relatives. "I think that covers all my family, but I have lots more back in town."

"So with all those preachers in your family, you still think of yourself as a prodigal daughter?"

"I *was!* I was rebellious and uncontrolled, but I'm one not any more. As soon as I get to feeling better, I'm gonna start helping Papa with the new mission work at Sandy Hill."

Jonathan patted her on the arm. "That's the best way to be. Don't let past mistakes get you down. I'll look for you to be in the congregation tomorrow."

Don't leave.

"How is the sermon coming?"

"I've got some questions I haven't settled, but I'm trusting the Lord to provide the answers."

"I'll let you know if I think the message is fitting for prodigals. I hope to be at church."

Maria's heart followed Jonathan as he walked away speaking to other folks.

What a blessing that Orville don't like me!

*   *   *

Sunday morning at church, Maria sat near the front so she wouldn't miss a word of the message. Grandpa, Tobias Grant, introduced Jonathan to the congregation. Before he sat down Tobias said, "We are blessed to hear the first sermon preached by this young man. Make a note in your Bible—the text for the first sermon by Jonathan Folsom.

"You old timers will remember my son, Samuel, preached his first sermon from that pulpit about sixteen years ago. It was on 'Vows'. Because of that sermon I surrendered to the ministry. Later, I preached my first sermon from there, too. God uses our church to introduce His men to the ministry from this stand." Tobias touched the smooth wood of the pulpit. He shook hands with Jonathan and took a seat behind him.

"How would you feel if a congregation of stoned-faced people stared at you for a half-hour?"

Giggles and laughs burst forth from the audience. Maria didn't laugh. This business was serious, but she realized Jonathan was trying to break the ice so folks would listen to God's Word.

"At least now some of the frozen faces have cracked and I see smiles on your faces. It's easier to preach when you seem happy."

Jonathan lifted his Bible in the air, and said, "Today I want to talk about the Prodigal Son. Turn in your Bible to Luke 15:11 through 24."

Maria knew Jonathan was nervous because his voice trembled and he stumbled over a few simple words. *Dear Jesus, help him to be calm.*

After reading the Scripture, Jonathan prayed for inspiration from the Lord. Then he launched into the sermon. "Here we find a young man who owned almost every worldly possession he desired. Yet, there was a need in his life that couldn't be met. Many of us are in that situation today. Our bellies are full; we have clothes on our backs; a roof over our heads; but there's an empty space in our lives. Others of you may not have enough food to eat, clothes to wear, or a comfortable house. You still have a yearning for more than the necessities of life. We start searching for something to fill the emptiness . . . often we look in the wrong places.

"The Prodigal Son asked for his portion of the inheritance. His father gave it to him! A few days later, he took a journey into a far country. If his father were a symbol for God, we would say that the Prodigal was in a state of departure and distance from Him. His main sin was turning from God to seek his own path." Jonathan made a sweeping motion with his hand, as if the Prodigal were heading the wrong way.

"He wanted to live his way. He was enticed by the desire for pleasures in a far country. Most of us have never been to a far country, not even to California, but may I inform you that anywhere away from God is a far country. Even though we never travel a hundred miles from home, that doesn't keep us from being lured by the glitter of the world. Often, we step inside a business, say a honky-tonk, just to look around. Maybe we tell ourselves we're looking for a friend. Usually, we don't turn and leave without participating in the transgressions offered therein. We don't leave without tasting firewater!"

Jonathan shook his head in mock disbelief. "What? Most of you aren't drawn away by the pleasures of this life? Alcohol? Moonshine? Your neighbor's wife? Come on, be honest. Regardless of our financial situation, most of us want a taste of life in a far country. That act takes us away from God, the Father."

Boys? Love? Maria added silently.

"Next comes the spending state. The Prodigal wasted his substance in riotous living. We could call that wild living. If a person assumes that he has enough money to live any way he chooses and do it indefinitely, that tells us he hasn't grown up yet."

Maria's heartbeat quickened. She felt her face growing warm with embarrassment.

I assumed I had enough to live away from home indefinitely. I must not be grown up yet.

"When we are in a far country, we do things we wouldn't do in our own communities. Sin is regarded as a pleasure, but it's only for the moment. You commit sin; then you try to sleep. The night is really long as you lie there wishing you hadn't participated in sinful activities. You're out in a far country, and you did things you wouldn't do in your own hometown."

I didn't do them, but I wanted to. Oh, yes, I did tell a lot of lies.

"Then came the wanting state. The Prodigal spent all his money and he needed more to pay his expenses. His life had been like a bubble: iridescent, beautiful, illusive, and easily burst. His bubble was about to burst. Not even his basic needs were met. He wanted simple things just to survive. He needed food.

"He moved to the servile state. He joined himself to a citizen of that country and began working for him. He stooped to feeding pigs, which was an abomination to the Jews. He would have gladly eaten the husks from the pods the swine ate. Often, on this trip downward, we find ourselves participating in activities even servants wouldn't do. That happened to the Prodigal. He reached the bottom. He said, ' I perish . . . '

"That's when he came to himself. He woke up. He could expect no help from anyone. Those who stay in a far country are lost and dying."

That's what happened to me. I realized I couldn't do anything to save myself.

"That is when the Prodigal repented. He realized that his father's servants had better food than he did. He knew he couldn't ask to be restored as he was before; he simply wanted to be as a hired servant. A hired servant was taken on to work for one day at a time, but the Prodigal was willing to do that. If repentance is genuine, it will involve turning from sin and turning to God. True repentance caused the Prodigal to leave the pigpen and start toward his father.

"The Prodigal had been dead. He had been lost. He had been in a state of folly and craziness, but he came to himself. Yes, he woke up. He went home. His appearance had changed drastically from what it was when he left. Now, he was dirty, ragged, and penniless."

That describes me.

"His father's reaction completely surprised him. The father ran out to meet his son. A celebration followed with a fatted calf, the best robe, which stands for honor, a ring, which means authority, and a pair of shoes for those bare feet, meaning sonship. Add to that lively music and dancing. What a day of rejoicing for all except the older brother. He was jealous.

"That day the Prodigal realized that his father truly loved him in spite of the filthy state he returned in. As I pondered on this parable, I wondered, 'Was the Prodigal a Christian, going astray, or was he an unsaved person?' To that question I answer—the truths in this Scripture apply to Christians who have gone astray and to the lost who have never trusted in Jesus as Savior. For those of you who fit in either group—lost or straying, I plead with you to come home to Jesus."

Jonathan motioned for the song leader to come forward.

"I would like for the musician to lead us in the song, *Lord, I'm Coming Home.* If the Lord leads you to do so, come home today."

Maria found herself singing with the congregation. How true the words were!

"I've wandered far away from God, Now, I'm coming home; . . . "

The words became a prayer for her, "Lord, I'm coming home, never more to roam."

*   *   *

That afternoon after everyone had eaten his fill of *pishofa,* the family sat in the shade of pine trees at Tobias' house. Some words Tobias had spoken at church this morning jabbed at Maria's imagination. Papa's first sermon was on "Vows." Just what kind of vows? It must have been a powerful message God used to call Tobias to be a preacher.

"Papa, tell me about the sermon on Vows," Maria asked.

"You've heard the story about my papa being condemned to execution, right?"

"Yes."

"Papa was so glad to be freed from execution, he made a vow to give his first son to be a preacher or a missionary. When Toby and I were born, Grandma tied a red string around the wrist of the older baby, who was named Samuel. One day, your Aunt Hallie was playing with us and took the string off. She didn't know if she put it back on the right baby's wrist."

White Rabbit broke in. "When Papa got bit by a copperhead, Hallie was so scared she couldn't stop crying. She bawled so long we forced her to tell us what was wrong. She said that the baby with a red string might not be the firstborn, because she didn't know if she put it back on the oldest son. For a long time after that, no one knew who was Sammy and who was Toby."

"Sammy was not wanting to be the oldest one," Papa said, and then he chuckled. "He thought he got out of being a preacher, because he always said he was too bashful to get up and talk."

"When you were a tiny baby, Maria, I had a bad dream about you. Someone was trying to take a red string off your wrist," Sammy revealed.

"I didn't have a string on my wrist," Maria protested. "I'm not a twin."

"You're right. But how could I have those feelings of having a string taken off my wrist, if I hadn't lived through them when I was a baby?

"Before I knew what was happening, I woke up and found myself outside on the horse. Toby ran out and stopped me. He said he finished the dream and told me you were okay. I knew then I was the older son because I was so scared when I dreamed someone tried to take the string off your wrist. Nobody else would know the feeling unless he had gone through the same experience. I took that as a message from God that I was supposed to be a preacher. That's why my first sermon was about Vows."

"So you were offered to be a preacher because Tobias made a vow to the Lord?"

"That's right. That day I challenged everyone in the congregation who had made a promise to the Lord to come forward to pray about their vows."

"When Papa was in the war, he had promised the Lord he'd preach, but he never fulfilled his vow," White Rabbit explained. "He went forward that day and offered his life as a preacher. He's been preaching ever since." White Rabbit's smile revealed how grateful she was about Tobias' surrender to the ministry.

"Quite a few came forward that Sunday," Sammy said. "I took that as an affirmation that the Lord had called me to preach."

*   *   *

Sammy and Louisa found a house to rent in town. Caleb and Flodell lived nearby. While Maria was regaining her strength, she rested for long periods. Words she heard the last few days kept playing in her mind.

When you were a tiny baby . . . why wasn't Papa at home with Mama when I was a tiny baby?

Tobias preached his first sermon sixteen years ago. I'm sixteen. Were my parents married?

That story Granny Wade told Flodell bothered her, too. The girl who stayed at the cabin—that girl's papa was a preacher. She stayed at the cabin so she wouldn't disgrace her family.

Lots of things just didn't add up. She'd need to listen more carefully when adults huddled around talking quietly.

Chapter Fifteen

Maria didn't help with housework for a few more days. She rested and ate, read and thought, while recuperating from the weeks of starvation. She thought a lot about her family background. Lots of unanswered questions bothered her. She must listen to everything her family said when they didn't know she close by.

Gradually, she gained back her strength and was ready to help with the mission at Sandy Hill. On one of the trips to Sandy Hill, Papa suggested they stop to visit Gracie and Luther. When Papa parked at the edge of the lawn, Maria saw Gracie working in her flowerbeds. Gracie stood up, pushed back her bonnet, and walked toward them.

"Howdy! Haven't seen you passing by lately."

"We've had some personal problems," Sammy said. He glanced toward Maria and smiled. "But everything has worked out for the best. You know the Bible states: 'For we know that all things work together for good to them that love God, to them who are the called according to *his* purpose.'"

That's the verse I told Flodell about.

"Where is that verse found, Papa?"

"Romans 8:28. Why?"

"I tried to quote it to Flodell, but I couldn't get it right. I want to show it to her in the Bible."

"Sure wish I could believe that verse, Preacher," Gracie said. "I truly love Luther, but he makes life miserable for me when he's on a cheap drunk. I don't know where he is now, but all the fruit jars are missing. You know what that means." She wiped tears from her eyes.

"He's filling them up with moonshine?" Maria asked.

"That's my guess," Gracie said. "Y'all come in. I could stand to cool off for a while."

When Gracie opened the door, Teency jumped into her arms. She snuggled the dog close to her chest and smoothed her coat.

"Where's Tuffy?" Maria asked.

"He's back there laying by Luther's bed, protecting his clothes. Sometimes I think that dog is smarter than Luther." She laughed sarcastically. She turned to face Sammy. "What about all things working together for good, Preacher? Can I believe that verse?"

"We must remember life is not going to be a smooth road for Christians. We have problems just like everyone else, but if we handle them with prayer, they'll work together for good. In the first place, it says that this is for those who love God. That is a mighty big requirement. You must love God."

Sammy looked toward Maria and said, "Remember that when you are trying to explain the verse to Flodell."

He turned back to Gracie. "That knocks out a huge majority of folks. They don't love God. And it applies to those 'who are the called according to *his* purpose'.

"I could explain it with a Bible story. Several famous men in the Bible went through trials before they came out victorious. Daniel is one and Joseph is another. Yes, Joseph is a perfect example."

Maria was puzzled and it seemed that Gracie was, too. "Why all this talk about Daniel and Joseph? They lived thousands of years ago. How could that apply to me and Luther?" Gracie asked, wiping perspiration from her brow. "I'm wanting happiness with Luther. I'm wanting him to stop drinking and get a job." She gazed at the bare walls. "I'd even like to have flowered wallpaper covering the boards in this room."

Sammy laughed. "One thing for sure is that people haven't changed.

Joseph felt he was special because God gave him dreams. That caused his brothers to be jealous. They took cruel actions against him. Can you remember any of the bad things the brothers did to Joseph, Maria?"

"Yeah. They threw him in a pit."

"Sold him into slavery," Gracie added.

"Yes, I could list many problems Joseph endured. He was falsely accused by the leader's wife and that caused him to be thrown into prison. But eventually, he was released from prison and given a place of authority, second only to Pharaoh. Because of his influence, he was able to save his entire family. He told his brothers that God sent him before them to preserve them. Finally, he saw his father again. But he endured a lot of hardships before he reached that period in his life.

"Instead of a situation like Joseph's, you, Gracie, are trying to live in a state of happiness. Whatever you're seeking, there will be obstacles to overcome. I know you have plenty of them to deal with."

Gracie nodded and more tears welled in her eyes.

"But, Gracie, in your case, as with many of us, one of the obstacles is the problem of alcohol. That can't be overcome without getting drink out of your life."

"Did you ever live with a drunk?" Gracie asked. "Until you do, you don't know the half of the problem."

"No, I haven't lived in a home where alcohol is a problem. Thank the Good Lord!" answered Sammy. "The stumbling blocks to reaching your goal would probably be, that *should* Luther declare himself free from drink; he'd fall off the wagon several times before he stuck with his resolution.

"You would need to be there to support and encourage him to start over again. You'd need to let him know of your unconditional love for him. Both of you would have to back up and start over again several times. However, I believe the real problem is that Luther needs a new heart. He needs the Lord in his life. He'd have to start at the beginning."

Louisa nodded. "He's right, Gracie. Luther needs to be saved."

"You're probably right. I don't think a true Christian could sit around and drink booze all the time," Gracie said. The sweet smile returned to her face.

"Back to the verse," Sammy said, seriously. "'All things work together for good to them who love the Lord, and who are the called according to *his* purpose.' Every problem, every discouragement in life can work together to fulfill the purpose of God. We have to go down life's road overcoming one problem at a time to reach the goal. And it's the same with your marriage—one day at a time."

Before they left, Louisa told Gracie about Flodell's marriage to Caleb.

"Well, good for her! I hope that girl gets a chance at happiness. Her pa sure didn't help out any in that part of her life," Gracie said.

"She and Caleb are our neighbors, so we see each other real often," Louisa added. "There are so many lives that need mending. Flodell's pa is one and Luther is another one."

"And a lot of people who live at Sandy Hill," said Sammy. "Maybe we should go and see if any of the women have come to their meeting." He took Gracie's hand and squeezed it. "I'm going to be praying for Luther."

*   *   *

Maria really wanted to meet Jonathan's parents at Sandy Hill. Papa had met Jonathan's pa, Charles Folsom, on the first trip. He said Charlie wasn't interested in church and no other man showed an interest, either.

Starting a church at Sandy Hill is gonna be hard.

She had heard Papa say that they were going to try to present a need to the folks in the community. Maybe if they saw the needs of others; that would point out their needs as well.

Now that Maria was helping with the establishment of church services, Papa asked her about a need to be addressed by the citizens of

Sandy Hill. Her first thought was the plight of homeless people. She considered herself and Flodell as two former destitute girls.

Of course, that was my fault. Maybe it's Flodell's fault, too.

"Right now, I'd say the homeless," Maria said.

"I doubt there are many homeless people living around Sandy Hill, but that's a good idea for a larger city," Sammy said.

"But what about all the tramps who knock on doors, asking for a bite of food?"

"You're right, I agree," Sammy said. "However, there aren't any of those coming around Sandy Hill. They jump from trains when they stop in towns. Now think of another need."

"I think building a shelter for younger women would answer a real need. They can come from anywhere and stay there for a few months," Louisa said. "You could even birth the babies." She paused for a moment. "Say, that's an idea!"

"What kind of idea?" Sammy asked.

"If we had a building, even a tent, and once a week you could help sick or hurt folks."

"But he's not a doctor," Maria protested. "Wouldn't he be disobeying the law if he treated sick people?"

Louisa laughed. "I'm not wanting him to break the law. I'm thinking of problems like bandaging cuts and sores, pulling loose teeth, simple things that don't require a medical degree. Your papa knows how to do that."

"We don't have the money to do that, Louisa," Sammy objected.

"I figure somebody would be willing to help—like Doc Coleman," Louisa said.

"He might be willing to share his supplies with me," Sammy agreed. "Maybe the District Superintendent would help, too."

"Grandmother Folsom!" Maria yelled, causing Sammy to swerve in the middle of the road. Louisa turned to frown at Maria.

"What are you yelling about?" Louisa demanded. "You want to get us killed?"

Maria cowered down in the back seat and covered her face with her hands. "Sorry, Mama," she said peeking at Louisa through a slit between her fingers. "I was thinking of Jonathan's grandmother who belongs to a group called Ladies' Aid Society. They make baby clothes, and sew, and do things for needy folks."

"And what does that have to do with the people at Sandy Hill?"

"Mama, you and I can go visit Jonathan's grandmother and let her tell us about how the Ladies' Aid Society helps people."

"Not if you're going to scream and cause me to wreck this automobile," Sammy answered sternly.

"Calm down and we'll talk about it quietly," Louisa said.

"She could tell us how it works and maybe come to get us started. Oh, never mind. The next time I see Jonathan, I'll ask him about what his grandmother does.

"Papa could doctor the sick," Maria added, hurriedly. "Maybe someone could tell Bible stories to the kids while their mamas are seeing Papa. There's lots of things we could do to help. We just need a tent or a building of some kind."

"It's a good thought," Sammy agreed. "I got a lot of medical training from Doc Coleman the summer I worked for him."

"Is there a surgery you can perform to lower folks' voices?" Louisa asked, laughing.

Chapter Sixteen

A few weeks later, while Papa visited with the men at Sandy Hill, Maria, Mama, Flodell, and several women sat on colorful pieced quilts spread under a tree. While they visited, they tore rags into strips to be used for bandages. The women talked freely now that they had become acquainted with Maria and Louisa. Most already knew Flodell.

"I guess this is my last week to meet with y'all, because I'll be starting to school at Riverview," Maria said.

"Too bad," muttered Millie. "We'll miss you."

"If Mama and Papa come on a day when I'm not in school, I'll come with them, though."

"And I'll have to stop coming when the baby is born," Flodell added. "I'll be busy washing diapers and taking care of Junior."

"Junior?" Louisa asked.

"Just a guess," Flodell said, and then she laughed. "Caleb will sure be a good helper since he can't get around too much. He can sit and rock Junior while I work."

"There can be some good come out of everything, if we just look for it," Louisa commented. "If something special is going on out here, Caleb might be able to take care of the baby and you could ride with us."

Flodell nodded, "You're right. I would trust him with the baby. He's the best man I've ever met." When she saw Sammy walking up, she laughed and changed the statement. "He's *one of the best men* I've ever . . . "

"That shows the power of God in a person's life," Louisa interrupted. Getting the attention of the women, she added, "Ladies, the man Flodell is married to, used to be cruel and heartless. Some of you know what I'm talking about? I know about her husband because he lived with us as our brother till after I left home. Papa made us give in to his every whim."

"I'm sure it was hard," Sammy said, taking Louisa's hand. "You and your family knew how heartless he was but your papa wouldn't believe it until he saw it with his own eyes. It all worked out, though."

Flodell nodded in agreement. "The change in him was worth the wait. It's wonderful to be treated with respect. I don't know nothing about using good manners. I'm used to having to fight for ever thing I get."

"Your pa wasn't good to you, was he?" asked Millie. "We all know Boogie Estep. He's messed up a lot of the families around here with that moonshine he makes."

The other women nodded in agreement and murmured quietly.

Maria saw tears pool in Flodell's eyes. She nodded. "I'm sorry, but Papa made me do a lot of his dirty work around the place."

"You mean you had to do the hard jobs like lifting heavy loads?" a woman asked.

"No, things like hiding out and doing things in secret. I always felt so dirty after I went to bed at night," Flodell confessed. "It was hard to go to sleep because I knew the things I did wasn't right."

"The life you've lived can be useful in helping all of us," Louisa said. "We need to live through the rough times to be able to understand the feelings of others. When you experience trials first hand, you can help others going through the same problems."

"Lots of us can understand how hard Flodell and her ma have had it," Lena Jenkins added.

"Ladies, we stopped by to see Gracie Langley the other day," Sammy interjected. "She was asking me about the meaning of a Bible verse because she was discouraged with the way Luther acts."

"We understand that, too," Lena said.

"Yes. Luther causes her a lot of heartache. Gracie was wondering about the verse that says, 'All things work together for good to them that love God and are the called according to *his* purpose.' She was wondering how all things could work for good when she lives with a man like Luther. I tried to explain it, but now it makes more sense," Sammy said, enthusiastically. He picked up a bandage roll and tossed it in the air. "Even me going with Doc on his rounds! I believe my work with sick folks is going to be used for good. That verse is found it Romans 8:28."

"Most of us are ready to work for the Lord out here," Louisa said, looking at the women sitting under the tree. "We've been through training."

"I hid out in a closet for a few weeks. I know what it's like to be lonely and hungry," Maria said.

Sammy looked around the group. "Every one of you who has trusted the Lord as Savior is ready to start helping spread the Gospel around Sandy Hill," he said. Reaching into his shirt pocket he pulled out his New Testament.

"What does that mean?" Flodell whispered to Maria. "I never trusted the Lord."

Sammy looked toward Flodell and nodded, indicating he understood her concern. "While ago, you said you had a hard time sleeping at night after your pa made you sneak around and do bad things. Every one of us is like that. When we realize we are sinning against God—not just our parents—then the Holy Spirit reveals the sin to us."

I felt that way when I stayed in the closet. I was a Christian, but I knew I was sinning when I ran away from home, Maria thought.

Sammy thumbed through his New Testament and put his finger on a verse. "*For all have sinned, and come short of the glory of God;*'" he read. "Listen to the word, 'All', that's everyone. Another verse tells us that '*There is none righteous, no, not one.*'

"If we have all sinned and come short of the glory of God, we need to realize—" Sammy paused to turn pages—"*'For the wages of sin is death; but the gift of God is eternal life through Jesus Christ our Lord.'*

"There are consequences for sinning against God."

I know that. I almost starved to death, Maria thought.

She glanced at Flodell. She saw tears overflowing and trickling down Flodell's cheeks. Suddenly, Flodell arose from the pallet and walked over to sit in the car. Sammy's glance seemed a hint to Maria that she should stay near Flodell.

"What's wrong?" Maria asked, standing at the window of the car door.

"I've done exactly everything Sammy is talking about," she said, and sobbed for a few seconds. "I've sinned and I've come way short in my life."

"That's too bad," Maria said, "but it can be changed today, if you want to become a Christian."

"I want my baby to have a different kind of life from what I've lived." She covered her face with her hands and sobbed. Looking up, she asked, "Can God change a dirty person like me? I've been on the wrong path ever since I was old enough to know better. I've felt filthy for a long time."

Maria's heartbeat was so erratic, she wondered if her heart was about to stop. She knew, though, that it was because of Flodell's confession.

What do I say?

"I need to make things right with God. I need to become a Christian," Flodell continued, without waiting for a reply. "I want Him to come into my heart and live in me. I—want—to—be—a—good—wife—for—Caleb. He's too good to me."

"Listen. Papa's telling you what to do," Maria said. She nodded toward Sammy.

"*'But God commendeth his love toward us, in that, while we were yet sinners, Christ died for us,'*" Sammy read. "That means that Christ died for us before we had any goodness of our own. The wages of sin are already paid. We just have to accept the payment as a free gift."

Maria watched Flodell smile.

"Then the Bible tells us exactly what to do: '*That if thou shalt confess with thy mouth the Lord Jesus, . . .*'"

A look of horror covered Flodell's face. She covered her mouth with her hand for a second. "Does that mean I have to get in front of those women and tell ever bad thing I've done? That would be so embarrassing."

"Confessing the Lord Jesus means that you're telling another person that you believe in Jesus—you've taken Him as your Savior. You don't have to name the sins you've committed."

Maria heard an audible sigh escape from Flodell's mouth.

"You confess with your mouth '*. . . and believe in thine heart that God hath raised him from the dead, thou shalt be saved.*'

"The next verse makes that clear. '*For with the heart man believeth unto righteousness, and with the mouth confession is made unto salvation.*

'*For whosoever shall call upon the name of the Lord shall be saved.*'

"If you're sorry for your sin—that means repent and turn the opposite direction—you will change completely. It means you've put your faith and trust in God, and believed in your heart and confessed with your mouth, you're saved," Sammy said. "All of us who have done that will be the nucleus, the starting of a new church at Sandy Hill. Everybody who agrees with that say, 'Amen.'"

Maria listened to almost everyone affirm Sammy's proposal with a quiet "Amen."

Flodell scooted from the car and walked toward Sammy. "I trusted the Lord and I'm ready to be baptized," she said. "If I had a extra dress, I could be baptized in the creek today."

Sammy smiled. "We could probably borrow a dress for you, but I know you want Caleb to be here for the baptism. Right?"

Flodell gasped and covered her mouth. "Caleb! I forgot my husband. Yes, I want him to be here. So we can do that the next time we come."

"Let's decide on a date," Maria suggested. "I want to be here, so why don't you be baptized before school starts?"

The ladies and Sammy huddled together for a few moments, then they announced the date. "Next Sunday afternoon," Sammy said. "And after the baptizing, we'll have dinner on the grounds." He turned to Louisa to ask, "Would you lead us in a song before we dismiss?"

Louisa nodded and hummed a note. She started singing, "I will arise and go to Jesus." Almost everyone joined in the refrain. "He will embrace me in His arms: In the arms of my dear Savior, Oh, there are ten thousand charms."

My song, thought Maria. "That's what you just did. You arose and went to Jesus," she said to Flodell. "So did I, when I came back home."

"Thank you for taking me in, Maria," Flodell said, sniffing back tears. "I didn't know what to do when Eli kicked me out of that car. Y'all welcomed me into your homes and now I'm a different person." She hugged Maria and Louisa.

"Oh, I can't wait to tell Caleb. Junior will be born into a Christian home. Life will be so different from what it would have been if I had married Eli." She looked into the sky and exclaimed, "Thank You, Jesus!"

Sammy shook Flodelle's hand vigorously. "We left home with a lost sheep and now you've been found. Welcome to the fold." He walked around the group of women to shake the hand of each one.

Driving back toward Riverview, at times Sammy led out in singing. The group was different from the one who had driven to Sandy Hill a while before. Flodell was a new person.

They were getting close to the turnoff to Flodell's parents' house, when Sammy pointed up the road and said, "That looks like a goat coming down the road."

"Look at that man in the cart! A white goat is pulling him down the road!" Maria exclaimed.

"It's Luther," Flodell said, matter-of-factly. "He's going to the still to get a load of moonshine. If you look close, you'll see Tuffy with him."

Sammy pressed down on the foot feed. "We don't want to get tangled up with him right this minute."

"Lightnin' probably wouldn't bother us," Flodell said.

"Lightning?" Maria asked.

"Yeah. The goat's name is White Lightnin'," Flodell answered. She laughed. "I've heard about goats and sheep being different. Sammy said I was a sheep. Well, there's your goat."

*   *   *

On Sunday, a few members of Sammy and Louisa's families drove to Sandy Hill to attend Flodell's baptism. On the way to the service, Sammy stopped for Gracie. When Gracie walked out of the house, Maria noticed the sweet lady wore a dress sewed from floral print. She had braided her hair and the braids encircled her head. She had placed a red rose on either side of the braids. Gracie stopped for a moment to retrieve a fruit jar filled with a bright bouquet of flowers.

Caleb, Flodell, and Granny Wade rode with White Rabbit and Tobias. When Maria saw her grandpa she wondered, *Who's preaching in his place today?*

While Papa preached, Maria glanced at the flower-filled jar Gracie had set on a flat rock. Who would have thought of decorating the worship area with a bouquet? Gracie had a flair for bringing beauty with her wherever she went.

After the sermon was finished, Tobias led the onlookers in singing *Shall We Gather at the River,* while Papa and Flodell waded out into the water. When they were on solid footing, Papa nodded that he was ready to baptize Flodell. After he said a few words about baptizing Flodell, carefully, he lowered her into the waters. Louisa and Caleb stood at the creek bank with dry cloths to wrap around the water-soaked twosome. Then Sammy and Flodell stepped behind separately covered areas to change into dry clothes.

The baptismal service inspired Maria to want to bring more lost sheep into the fold. *Maybe I'll marry a preacher.* The only unmarried preacher she could think of was Jonathan Folsom. Jonathan! Did he preach for Grandpa today? Did she miss out on the chance to see Jonathan and hear his sermon?

After the closing prayer, Maria hurried over to ask Grandpa who was preaching for him.

"That young man who preached right after you came home. His name is Jonathan Folsom, I think," Tobias answered. He winked at her and grinned. His smile showed he knew Maria liked Jonathan. "Remember him?" he asked, followed by a laugh. His loud chuckle embarrassed Maria.

Is there a way I can see Jonathan while he's here? Will he preach tonight?

The dinner wasn't nearly as appetizing to Maria as it would have been, if she hadn't known Jonathan was around. Now her feet itched to get back to Riverview, but she knew giving way to those feelings could lead to disaster. She must be patient.

While she waited for her parents, Maria watched Caleb and Flodell laughing and teasing each other. Caleb had been so transformed since he became a Christian; everyone said it was miraculous. She kept glancing at the couple. She hoped no one saw her staring, but she marveled at how blessed Caleb was to have married Flodell. She had completely changed, too.

Will my marriage be as happy as theirs?

It seemed to Maria that Papa would never get ready to leave. Did Papa know Jonathan was in Riverview? Was he dragging along on purpose? She went to sit in the car, hoping Papa would notice her and tell Mama and Gracie he needed to leave. She rested her head on the back of the seat, wishing to take a nap. Time would go faster while she slept.

She had not fallen asleep when she felt a gentle touch on her shoulder. She opened her eyes to see Jonathan's smiling face.

Maria's heart skipped a beat.

"Halito," Jonathan said. "Are you too sleepy to talk?"

"No," Maria answered. She covered her mouth, pretending to yawn.

I can't let him know my real feelings.

"Why are you taking a nap?" Jonathan asked. "You should be out talking to everyone."

"I'm ready to leave. I thought maybe Papa would notice me in the car and tell Mama he wanted to go home," Maria answered.

I can't tell Jonathan I wanted to see him.

"Would you like to get out and walk around, so you can wake up?" Jonathan asked, opening the door for her.

"Yes," she replied. Now that she and Jonathan were face to face, she couldn't think of any words to say.

While they walked along the sandy road, Jonathan talked about his aspirations to become a preacher. Suddenly, he stopped, turned to her and asked, "How has the Prodigal Daughter been getting along? Are you living up to your promise to be more obedient?"

Maria nodded. "I'm trying real hard."

"You sure do look better than you did that day on the train." His smile seemed to melt any reservations separating them.

"I was worse off than I thought. Doing without food and sleeping on the closet floor almost made me sick," Maria confessed.

"So, what did you do to recuperate?"

"I lay around and rested for several days. I did lots of thinking about life. I studied some. It took a while to get back to normal. Once I got back to my natural self, I've been riding out here with my parents every time they come."

"I'm glad your papa is working out here. My parents really need the Lord."

Jonathan gazed toward a house on down the road. He exhaled a long sigh.

"What else are you doing, now that you're well?"

"I'll be starting to back to school soon."

"You have a feller at school?"

Maria felt her face growing warm with shame. She struggled to find the exact words to answer. She stopped to face Jonathan. Putting her hands on her hips, she looked him directly in the face. "Don't you remember when we were on the train I told you I ran away because of a boy? He was the last boy I was sweet on . . . "

That's not true. I'm struck with Jonathan.

Jonathan grabbed Maria's hand, pulling her to the shade of tree, as a car drove by.

Is Papa looking for me?

They stood beneath the tree while Maria tried to finish the sentence. "It'll be hard to trust another boy," she said.

But you're not a boy, you're a man, she wanted to add.

"I need to start back to the car," Maria said. *But I don't want to.* "Papa may be ready to leave. Was he driving by?" She pointed down the road.

"No. That was a different kind of car," Jonathan answered. "But we'll start back anyway. I don't want your pa to get upset with me for walking you too far down the road." He turned loose of her hand as they drew closer to the crowd.

"I hope to see you whenever I'm in Riverview or here at Sandy Hill," he said. "What's your address? I may write you a letter."

Does he really mean that?

"Just send it to General Delivery, Riverview. I'll get it at the post office."

"I'll put my address on the letter I send you, then you can write back." Jonathan looked deeply into Maria's eyes and asked, "Be my angel while I'm gone. Okay?"

Maria felt a warm feeling overflowing from her heart and into her entire body. She couldn't speak audibly; she just shook her head up and down.

Yes, yes, yes! Preachers need angels.

Chapter Seventeen

$\mathcal{E}$very time Sammy and Louisa drove to Sandy Hill, Maria secretly hoped they'd return with news of seeing Jonathan Folsom. She always asked questions of Mama such as: "Who came to the women's meeting? Was a new person there? Did Papa see Charlie Folsom? Did Charlie's wife come to the meeting?"

Mama always answered, "No."

It would be more satisfying to Maria than eating a dish of vinegar pie to get close to a young man who was considerate, kind, and well behaved—every trait that Jonathan seemed to possess. What did he mean when he said, "Be my angel while I'm gone. Okay?" Maybe he said that to all the girls. Perhaps Maria should forget about Jonathan and pay attention to the boys at school who seemed interested in her. They were so immature! Jonathan was more grown up and serious. His ambition to become a preacher touched a cord deep in her heart. Maybe he would behave like Papa.

After school each day, Maria stopped at the post office to see if she had a letter from Jonathan. At last, the postmaster held out a letter for her. She looked at the perfect handwriting to read her name: "Maria (Angel) Grant." She felt her face burning with embarrassment. Jonathan remembered! He asked her to be his angel while he was away. She tucked the precious letter inside the top of her dress. She raced home to read it while she was alone.

Hope nobody's here.

She ran up the steps and into the front room. "Mama," she called. No answer. "Papa," she yelled. Still, no one replied. Smiling to herself, Maria walked into her room, closed the door, and fell across the bed. She pulled the letter from the top of her dress and stared at the writing for a few minutes. "Maria (Angel) Grant." Maybe Jonathan would go into more details inside the letter about what he meant by calling her "Angel." She tore the end off the envelope. A picture of Jonathan fell out. She gazed at the picture of him dressed in a white shirt and a suit. His black hair was pulled straight back from his forehead, combed in pompadour style. His smiling face stared back at her.

"He is so handsome!"

Opening the page she read:

"Dear Maria,

"Sadly and regretfully, I ask you to forgive me, Angel . . . "

For what?

". . . for not having written sooner, but I had a stack of lessons to get caught up on when I returned to school."

You're forgiven.

"I'll be getting a teaching certificate at the end of this semester if I can fulfill all the requirements. My goal is to start teaching and I can be a preacher, too."

Does a preacher need a wife?

"I don't think I'll get to come back to Riverview any more until school is out in January. We'll have to keep in touch by writing letters.

"In the meantime, could you send me your picture so I can look at it every day?"

Maria dropped the letter to start looking for a picture. If she could find the one she wanted, she'd mail it back today. After she found the picture, she picked up Jonathan's letter to continue reading:

"I wrote a poem for you. Tell me if you like it."

Maria

An angel is flying through the starry night
I can't look for her, because I have to write.
So I'll keep her picture on the desk by a book,
And ever so often, I'll take a look,
To keep her sweet face fresh in my mind.
Have to study this lesson; can't get behind.
So Angel, fly around while I read,
Your lovely presence will fill the need
That's in my heart to see your dear face,
I'll look at your picture to fill the empty space.

"I'm sending my picture so you can remember me.

"Sincerely,
"Jonathan Folsom."

"That is so romantic!" Maria said. She turned onto her back and hugged the letter to her breast. She touched the picture to her lips.

Be careful, Maria. Don't get involved with a boy you can't trust.

"I can trust Jonathan," she said aloud. "I've got to write him a letter right now." She pulled a sheet of paper from her schoolwork and started scribbling. She wrote, "I got the sweetest letter from you today. I have not thought of anything but you for days." She wrote every romantic sentence she could think of. All the sweet things she had believed about Orville before he showed his true self. Between every other sentence she inserted, "I love you." Then she wrote, "You're the only thing I have worth living for."

When she picked up the pages of Jonathan's letter to read again, she felt like she had been scolded. He didn't say, "I love you" one time. He just wanted her picture.

With tears stinging her eyes, she put the letter aside and decided to wait to mail it. She might change her mind. Maybe she wasn't as much in love with Jonathan as she imagined.

The next day, while sitting in math class, she doodled on a blank sheet of paper. To keep from forgetting about the lesson she learned from her infatuation for Orville Maria wrote, "O. S. loves M. G." inside a heart. A flood of shame washed over her. Orville turned out to be a shame in her life. Instantly, she put a big X though the heart. She hoped she never made such a foolish mistake again. Would her fascination with Jonathan turn out to be the same? In spite of the resistance she felt, she wrote, "M. G. loves J. F." inside a fancy heart. That made more sense. To get her mind off Jonathan, she wrote the initials "L. D. L. loves L. A. L." and drew a heart around them.

Who is L.D.L.? If he's Austin's pa, he has to be Indian.

But a moment later, her thoughts returned to Jonathan.

I'll write another letter but I won't tell him I love him.

While Maria walked to the next class, a boy stepped beside her. He whispered, "Do you have a feller?"

Maria felt her face burning with embarrassment. "No!" she said and walked faster.

The boy caught up with her. "I saw you writing initials in hearts back in class. I wondered if any of those letters were yours and your feller's."

"No! I was just playing around wasting time," Maria answered, but her conscience bothered her. "Well, some were mine. I put the initials of a has-been with mine to see how stupid it looked. It was ridiculous."

"A 'has-been'? You mean you don't like him any more?"

"Exactly. He doesn't even live here. He's out of my life for good."

"Could I walk with you to class?"

"If we're going to American History."

"A different class," the boy said. "Maybe I'll see you tomorrow." He smiled and turned to go the other way.

Not for any thing involving love.

Maria touched the picture of Jonathan she had tucked inside her pocket and hurried to her next class. It clung to her hand like a warm magnet. Perhaps the emotion she felt was true love.

Later, while Maria sat in study hall, she wrote another letter to Jonathan. She told him news of the meetings at Sandy Hill; wrote about her family; Flodell and Caleb and other folks he had met. She mentioned having seen Luther in the cart pulled by White Lightning. As much as she yearned to, she did not write of her deep love for Jonathan. She put the picture of herself in the envelope, sealed it and got it ready to mail when she left school. She wanted to apply lipstick and kiss the flap, and write "SWAK," sealed with a kiss, but she decided against it. What if the letter was returned and Papa saw it?

She felt deep regret when she stepped inside to post office. She wanted Jonathan to know of her love, but loathed the idea of becoming so infatuated with him that she'd run away and hide in a closet to be near him. An acknowledgment of true love must come later.

Chapter Eighteen

*M*aria finished washing the dishes after supper. She shook the crumbs from the tablecloth and put away the dishcloth.

"I can't stop seeing the picture of Luther sitting in that cart pulled by White Lightning," Louisa commented, arranging a bowl of pine cones the table. "How can Gracie put up with Luther delivering moonshine to folks who are already down and out?"

"Only by pure love for the man and love for the Lord," Sammy answered.

Does real love overlook bad sins like that? Maria wondered.

"She must really love Luther," Maria said.

A loud knocking at the door interrupted the conversation. Maria stepped to the door to welcome Caleb and Flodell.

Sammy stood up and walked out to shake hands with Caleb. "Why don't we sit outside? It's cooler out here," he said, leading the way to the chairs lined on the porch. "Have a seat. We were just discussing Luther and White Lightning," he said, offering a chair to Flodell. "How did Luther ever marry such a sweet wife as Gracie?"

Flodell shrugged her shoulders. "Who knows?" she asked. "I hear tell he used to be really handsome when he was a young brave."

"I never was handsome," Caleb said. "How did I get such a sweet wife as you?" He pinched Flodell on her cheek.

Flodell smiled tentatively. "I haven't always been 'sweet'. Hopefully, I'm learning more about being loveable."

"Neither one of us started off loveable."

"The Lord can take a dark sinful person and give him a pure heart," Sammy said. "Just think. My pa was condemned to execution. The Lord saved his soul and freed him from the death sentence. Later, Papa surrendered to be a preacher. He's the pastor right over there." Sammy pointed toward the church a few blocks away.

"He *is* now," Louisa said. "It looks like Jonathan Folsom is wanting to take his place." She winked at Sammy.

How dare Mama say that?

"You know that's not true, Mama," Maria objected. "He just preached for Grandpa so Grandpa could go to Flodell's baptizing."

"Your mama was just teasing," Sammy said.

She'd better be.

"I'm glad your family came to my baptizing. None of mine came, that's for sure," Flodell said. She paused for a moment, as if trying to say more. Finally, she asked, "You know, I was telling about my pa making me do bad things before I met y'all?"

All the listeners nodded in agreement.

Flodell pointed northward toward the edge of town. "I used to do some of that work back over there." Her lips quivered and it seemed to Maria as if Flodell was about to cry.

"I used to be like Luther—I delivered white lightnin' for Pa."

"In a cart pulled by a goat?" Maria asked loudly.

Did she really do that?

"No. I told y'all I was sneaky, remember?"

"In what way?" Maria asked.

Flodell hesitated. "This is really hard to confess. Sammy, you read that Bible verse about confessing? I'm sure glad I didn't have to tell everybody at the meeting, but Papa forced me to do things I despised doing."

"You don't have to tell us, if you don't want to," Sammy said, quietly.

"At the risk of being kicked out of the family, I'll tell y'all," Flodell said. She twisted her hands in her lap, then, she burst out, "Papa asked a woman to let me use her baby. I'd wrap up my friend's baby in a blanket and pretend to be walking downtown. But inside that blanket I'd hide a jar of white lightnin' I was taking along to sell."

"You didn't!" Louisa exclaimed.

"Yes, I did," Flodell confessed. "Oh, I didn't want to do it, but Papa made me. I was on pins and needles; afraid I'd drop the baby and the jar. I couldn't get out of it. Eli took me to town and let me out at this woman's house. Then I got the baby and walked toward town. There were plenty of men wanting to buy moonshine. I did that at night when Papa had a batch of white lightning ready to sell. Those are the nights I couldn't sleep. I'm forgiven and now I sleep real good."

"Praise the Lord!" Sammy said.

"Yeah, me too" Caleb said.

Maria swallowed back the agitation juggling around inside her. The love of God had to be big to forgive sins caused by the moonshine business.

"And if I had married Eli, who knows how my life would have turned out?" Flodell asked. "Worse than Gracie's, I'm sure. Now, life gets better every day, because God gave me a sweet husband." She smiled at Caleb.

"You two are good for each other," Louisa agreed.

"Yeah, Caleb takes over when I don't feel good. He can do housework better than I can," Flodell bragged. "Course, I worked with Pa. I didn't help in the house so I didn't have any experience. Caleb's teaching me."

"Don't know how long it'll take her to learn to wash dishes," Caleb teased.

The talk turned to lighter subjects, but Maria couldn't shake the thoughts about making and selling moonshine.

It makes people act stupid. Sure glad Jonathan isn't a drunk.

*   *   *

One afternoon, after school dismissed for the day, Maria rode with her parents to Sandy Hill. Papa drove to Gracie's house to park beside the garden fence. Gracie stood, and rubbed the small of her back. She pulled back her bonnet and welcomed her friends with a big smile. She beckoned them to follow her into the house.

"Have a seat," she said. "I'll get us a drink of water."

While Gracie was out of the room, Maria stared at the horizontal boards covering the wall. A picture of Jesus adorned the wall: nothing more.

Jesus is all I need. Yeah, I would like Jonathan, but . . .

Gracie returned with the water bucket and a granite dipper. Teency followed behind her.

"Where's Tuffy?" Maria asked.

"Out with his master," Gracie said, handing a dipper of water to Sammy. "Heaven only knows where they are." She set the bucket on a table and motioned for all to partake of the cool water. "He's getting worse, Brother Grant. He's either drinking or over at the still helping Boogie brew more moonshine. Comes in at all hours of the night, falling over the furniture. I can't keep things straightened up when he's here, except when he's in bed sleeping. He does sleep a lot, though."

"Why don't you ride to Sandy Hill with us? That way you can get your mind off Luther," Maria said. "Is that okay with you, Papa?"

"Sure," Sammy said. He turned to Grace. "If you want to go, we'll walk out and look at the flowers while you get ready."

Gracie arose and started pulling off her apron. "I think I'll take you up on that. I need to see some more cheerful faces."

The Grants walked out to the neatly kept flower garden. Maria gazed at the varieties of plants growing that were unfamiliar to her. She recognized zinnias and petunias, but not many other flowers. Roses, of course, she thought, gazing at the roses climbing up wires fastened to the house. Everyone knew about roses. Traditionally, folks wore them decorating their clothes when they went to church on Mother's Day; those whose mothers were living wore red; those whose mothers had passed on wore white. She quickly dismissed the thought about loved ones passing on.

The part of the garden that always caught her attention most was the rock path leading from the gate to the porch. Someone—probably Gracie—had placed rocks and stones of different sizes, shapes, and shades in creative designs. No grass sprouts marred the spaces between the rocks. On either side of the rock path, grew a row of moss plants in a rainbow of colors. The arrangement must have taken a long time to set the rocks in place.

Doubtless, Gracie tugged the heavy rocks fitting them side-by-side, before she decided exactly how to match them together. Too bad Gracie didn't have children; they would have enjoyed skipping on the rock path.

In a few minutes, Gracie stepped out the front door carrying Teency. "Is it okay if I take my dog with me?" she asked.

Sammy nodded and motioned toward the car. "Let's be going. We don't have too long before dark."

The meeting at Sandy Hill went well. Sammy taught the women and children a Bible lesson. Then the women visited and laughed while they rolled strips of cloth for bandages.

On the way home, Sammy turned the headlights on, because it was growing dark. He drove the car close to the picket fence at Gracie's house to let her and Teency out. No lights shined from the window, so Luther must not have returned home.

"Thanks for taking me with you," Gracie said. "I enjoyed going."

"We'll wait while you go in and light the lamp," Sammy said. "Then we'll leave."

In a few minutes, Maria saw the flicker from a coal oil lamp shining through the window. Papa drove onto the main road to continue the trip back home.

"Next time, we need to leave earlier," Papa said. "I don't like to drive on these sandy roads in the dark. What if we had a flat or the motor got hot or I slid off in a ditch?"

"We just have to trust we'll get home safely," Louisa said.

Carefully, Sammy steered the wheels inside the sandy ruts. As they neared the main road, Maria was about to expel a big breath of relief, when she saw a strange form in the road.

"What's that up the road?" she asked.

Papa started slowing down the car as they approached the figure. "Don't know what it is, but it looks like a person lying in the road," he replied.

As they drew closer, Maria saw a small black animal dancing around a larger shape. A black hat looked as if it had been tossed into the middle of the road. Then Maria shivered as her eyes made out the figure of a body! A human being lay stretched out on the road! An Indian wearing clothes that looked like Luther's lay there. The stranger was Luther! A shiver ran up her spine. She hugged herself as she began to tremble.

"Papa," she screamed, "that's Luther Langley! Tuffy's trying to wake him up."

"If that don't beat the hens 'a peckin'," Louisa said. "Luther's out on the road, drunker than a skunk."

"You're right, Louisa," Sammy said, driving to the edge of the road. "That's our friend Luther and his dog."

"What do we do?" Maria asked.

Poor Gracie.

"That remains to be seen. If we can pick him up, we'll take him back home, and get him out of danger. I think we can push him in the front seat. Louisa, you'll need to ride in the back. First, I'm going drive up the road a ways and turn around, so we'll be headed back to Gracie's."

In a few moments, the car was facing the south, toward Luther's house. Everyone got out of the car. They walked over to Luther and stood gazing at his limp form. Tuffy hopped around and put up a fuss. Maria knew the dog was trying to protect his master.

"We've got to get Luther in on Mama's side of the car." Sammy circled Luther's body, assessing the situation. "Let's see. If I pick up his arms and upper part of his body, y'all can each one lift a leg. We may have to drag him to the car door."

Tuffy snapped at Sammy as the man leaned over Luther's limp form. "Tuffy's sure trying to protect Luther," Sammy commented. "Okay, grab hold of his legs, and let's pull him to the car."

Moonshine is rotten.

Maria and Louisa tugged at Luther's legs. Papa pulled his arms and shoulders. Slowly, they inched him through the sand toward the car door. Maria tried to wipe off the grains of sand clinging to Luther's clothes while Papa walked to his side of the car.

"I'm going to get inside the car and pull him in from there," Sammy said. "Y'all push the best you can. Let's just get him in; doesn't matter how he fits. He's dead to the world, anyway."

After a while of pushing and tugging, Luther lay slouched inside the car. Tuffy jumped in after him. Maria walked back to grab Luther's hat. Then she and Louisa squeezed into the backseat, and Papa drove off. "We're going to let him out at the garden gate so he can sober up. Tuffy will guard him."

"What about Gracie? Shouldn't we tell her?" Louisa asked.

"If she's still up, we will," Sammy said.

When the car pulled into the yard, Maria looked for a light inside the house, but it was already out. Sammy stopped and got out. He went to Louisa's side of the car and pulled Luther out. Tuffy jumped out and stood guard over Luther. Sammy walked to the garden gate and hung the black hat on a fence post.

Soon, the Grant family was on their way home again. Sammy sighed. "I sure feel sorry for Gracie when she finds Luther stretched out beside the fence," he said.

"But she'll be relieved to know that he's safe, anyway," Maria said.

Maria couldn't get the scene of Luther's drunken body lying across the road out of her mind. What if a driver had been going fast and didn't see him? Luther would have been smashed.

Drinking alcohol is a curse.

*   *   *

A few days later, Maria accompanied her parents to visit Gracie. Sammy wanted to tell Gracie about finding Luther stretched out across the road. Maybe, he'd give her a warning to be on the lookout for her husband.

Seated in the simple front room, Maria recognized the difficulty Sammy faced trying to bring up the subject of Luther's problem. He shifted in his chair, cleared his throat a few times, and crossed and uncrossed his legs.

I think Papa needs help. Just as well get things started.

"How's Luther's drinking problem?" Maria asked.

"No better; maybe worse," Grace answered. "He came back sometime in the night after you brought me home last week. I found him in the yard the next morning."

"Gracie," Sammy said slowly and deliberately, "we brought Luther home. We found him—"

"You don't mean it!" Gracie exclaimed. She covered her face with her hands.

"He was out cold. Never knew when we put him in the car and brought him back," Sammy added. "Something needs to be done, or he'll end up dead."

"I could say I'm surprised, but I'm not," Gracie said, wiping tears from her eyes. "He's passed out on the roadside several times lately. Just as well brace myself for the worst."

"Luther needs to be saved. I'm not saying that'll cause him to quit drinking, but . . . " Sammy said. "He needs to make peace with God."

There was a noise at the front door. Maria glanced up to see what caused it when Luther staggered in. Gracie jumped from her chair and rushed to help Luther get inside.

"Maybe y'all should leave," she said, softly. "It'll take a while for Luther to sleep off this drinking spree." She opened the door for the Grants to walk out.

As they stepped out, Luther yelled, "I'll be at church Sunday."

Passionately, Maria's heart rate jumped to high gear. Luther said he'd come to church!

When the family sat safely in the car, Maria asked, "Did you hear that, Papa? Luther's coming to church Sunday!"

"Yeah, I heard. I've heard drunks promise that many a time. After they get sober, they forget all about it."

"Oh," Maria said. "Is that what they do?" She sighed in disappointment.

"We must pray that Luther will accept the Lord as Savior," Louisa said.

"That is the truth," agreed Sammy.

Chapter Nineteen

$\mathcal{F}$all shoved its way toward winter. The weather turned bitterly cold early that year. Maria spent the long cold nights snuggled in bed, dreaming about Jonathan. He wrote that he'd complete the required classes to obtain a life teacher's certificate in January, if he could just keep his nose to the grindstone. When he received the certificate, he'd be looking for a teaching position but few schools needed a teacher at midterm unless a teacher became ill or one died. Maria certainly didn't want anyone to get sick or die, but she hoped Jonathan could find a position in a school district somewhere near her area. He could help Grandpa Tobias with the church at Riverview.

In her letters, Maria wrote about her parents continuing to travel to Sandy Hill for church services when the weather permitted. She related how they counted it a victory to conduct services in Lena's house on cold days. She advised Jonathan of her parents' eagerness to encourage the ladies as they sought out a place set up for Sammy to do medical work. Never did she reveal to Jonathan her growing love for him. Best wait till they looked into each other's eyes. Would Jonathan's eyes reveal his love for her?

She wrote that her parents had taken Luther home when they found him passed out on the road . . . of Luther's desperate need for the Lord in his heart and life.

Always, Jonathan expressed concern for the Christian work at Sandy Hill and for the most crucial need in Luther's life. Through the exchange of letters, Maria became better acquainted with Jonathan. Several times he asked about Flodell and Caleb. He seemed interested in them because he attended their wedding at the cabin.

One night, Maria sat in the corner of the front room, writing a letter to Jonathan. She wrote about how Flodell seemed to be getting physically weaker all the time. Caleb had taken on more of the housework until he did most all of it now. She mentioned her uneasiness about Flodell's physical condition. Maria looked up to see Louisa standing in the doorway of the kitchen. A look of concern covered her face.

"Papa and I are going over to Gracie's. Papa's worried that Luther hasn't come home. If he's passed out on the road somewhere, he could freeze to death tonight. Do you want to go or stay here where it's warm?"

I should go. I might spot Luther.

"I'll go." Maria arose to take the letter writing material to her room. She hid it under her pillow. She found a pair of overalls and a heavy top to slip into. She grabbed her coat off the hook on the wall and pulled a cap, and mittens from the pockets. In a few minutes, the family was heading toward the turnoff that led to Sandy Hill.

"What's going on?" Maria asked.

"Nothing that I know of," Sammy answered, "but when I was by Gracie's late this afternoon, she said Luther had been gone all day. I'm afraid he's passed out and is somewhere stretched across the road or, even worse, fell into a ditch. I'll feel better if I know he's at home, sober or drunk."

"You don't have anything to go on, do you? You're just concerned?"

"Yeah, that's it," Louisa answered.

After Sammy turned off the main road onto the sandy trail, he inched along slowly. "Louisa, you look on the right side and Maria, you look on the left side watching for Luther," he said. "I don't know whether Tuffy is with him or not."

In spite of everyone paying careful attention looking for Luther's figure on the road, he wasn't found. Sammy drove the car beside the picket fence at Gracie's. "Let's go in," he said.

Gracie walked out the door carrying the lamp before the visitors knocked on the door. One look at her face told Maria Luther hadn't come home. "Oh, I'm so glad to see you," Gracie said. "I'm worried about Luther. He's not here, and it's way below freezing. What do I do?" She held the door open, inviting them inside.

"He's not on the road anywhere between here and the cut off, either," Sammy said. "Does he usually stay away as long as he has today?"

Gracie smiled apologetically. "Not really, but it's my fault. I talked real seriously about his need for the Lord in his life before he left. It's because I'm concerned about him." She pushed a wisp of hair behind her ear. Maria watched a tear trickle down Gracie's cheek. Her heart skipped a beat as she listened to Gracie say, "Luther got mad at me. He said he didn't want any 'lost sinner' sermons preached at him. He packed up and stomped out in a huff. I haven't seen him since."

Louisa gave Gracie's arm a squeeze. "What you did was right. Don't worry about it. Luther's probably off somewhere thinking about the things you said." She turned to Sammy and asked, "You think so, Sam?"

"Yes. You did the right thing. Let me warm up a minute and think about what I should do." He held his hands up to the pot-bellied heater. "It's too cold for Luther to be out there tonight. That's what I'm worried about."

Maria watched the expression on Gracie's face. The shadows cast by the dim lamplight emphasized the lines of concern etched in her face.

"Luther causes me a lot problems, but I love him even more because of that. I *have* to love him because most everyone else despises him. He can't live without love."

"Where's Tuffy?" Maria asked. The somber conversation made her feel squeamish.

"He's with Luther," Gracie whispered, holding back a sob. "I'd sure hate to lose that faithful little dog, too. He's Luther's best friend." She covered her face with both hands and wept softly.

Louisa patted Gracie's back. "Sammy will try to find him," she murmured.

"Yeah. I need to know where to start," Sammy said. He paced back and forth for a few moments, then stopped and turned to Louisa. "Why don't you stay with Gracie? Maria can ride with me. She can look on one side of the road and I'll look on the other."

"Is there any reason Luther would go south toward Sandy Hill?"

"Yes. Some of his old cronies live down that way," Gracie replied. "You know that by the way Millie and Lena talk about Boogie. Luther and Boogie mean the same to them—moonshine."

Sammy grabbed his coat and pulled it on. Maria slipped hers on, too. Sammy started toward the door, motioning for Maria to follow him. "If we don't come back in—say an hour—we may be in trouble. We're headed south. Y'all pray while we're gone."

"Be careful, Sam," Louisa warned, following the two out the door. "Maria, don't you take any risks out in this freezing weather."

Sammy and Maria climbed into the car and Sammy drove out of the yard. "Keep your eyes on the right side. I'll watch the left," he advised. He started humming *Amazing Grace,* as he drove along.

No unusual objects cluttered the sandy road. Occasionally, a dead leaf sailed across in front of the car.

Probably all the wild animals are holed up tonight because it's too cold for them to be out.

"Was this morning the last time anybody saw Luther?" Maria asked. She pulled her coat closer around her body. Staying out in this weather would cause frostbite for sure, and most likely death.

"Gracie said he left home this morning and didn't come in to eat or feed the stock," Sammy answered. "Must have been nipping moonshine all day to keep warm."

Sammy drove by Boogie Estep's house. Maria looked at the path leading to his residence. "Sure a lot of misery takes place at that house and the still," Sammy commented as he drove by.

"I'll never forget how mean Boogie treated Flodell the day he kicked her out," Maria reminisced.

"What were you doing here?" Sammy demanded.

How do I tell this without lying?

"Sheriff Lincoln drove Flodell out to get her clothes. White Rabbit and I rode with them. You know, you and Mama went to the Preachers' Conference. I was staying with White Rabbit when Flodell came and asked Grandpa to take her home, but he'd already gone to the cornfield. We asked the sheriff to take us over here."

"Sometimes good comes out of bad. I'm glad you met Flodell. She became a Christian and is ready for the next step in her life," Sammy said. "But you don't need to have any dealings with Boogie—he's bad medicine."

"I learned my lesson," Maria confessed. She wanted to get on another subject, quick. "Should you drive back in the woods looking for the still?"

"I should, but I don't know where to find it. We could get lost or the car could run off in a ditch. No," Sammy said, shaking his head. "If we don't find Luther tonight, maybe somebody will go to the still tomorrow. It's too dangerous out in this cold. Your mama said for you not to take any risks."

Risky whiskey.

Sammy sped up just a smidgen, but not too fast to overlook noticing a human being lying near the road. He began to hum *Amazing Grace* again. He drove to Shady Hill without any sign of Luther. Most all the lamps had been blown out, indicating folks were in bed for the night. By the beams of the headlights Maria saw smoke curling from the chimneys of most homes.

I'm sure glad Gracie talked to Luther about Spiritual things. Maybe he's out thinking about what she said.

"It looks like Luther isn't passed out on the side of the road," Sammy said. "We'll go back to Gracie's."

Maria felt anxiety fluttering in her breast when she thought about Luther and Tuffy still missing. Should they give up the search as soon as this?

Sammy drove faster on the return trip, but Maria kept her gaze on the road. Luther could have stumbled out of the woods after they drove by.

Almost to Grace's, Maria saw a small black dog trotting through the sand. Tuffy! "Papa, stop! That's Tuffy."

Sammy stopped the car. Maria jumped out to rescue the dog. He didn't resist her touch. Gingerly, she picked him up and crawled back inside the car. While getting Tuffy seated in her lap, Maria's hand touched a coarse piece of cloth fastened onto the strip of leather around Tuffy's neck. Her heart jumped with hope. "Stop, Papa! Something's tied to Tuffy's neck."

Sammy stopped the car. He and Maria jumped out and walked to the front of the car. Maria held Tuffy near the headlights so they could see what was attached to the leather strip. It appeared to be a scribbled one-word message. Maria couldn't make out the word. She held the cloth closer to Sammy for him to read.

"H-m-m-m. It says 'Jesus'."

What does that mean?

They got back inside the car. Sammy started driving toward Gracie's.

Luther was alive when he wrote "Jesus."

"So what do you think the word 'Jesus' means?" Maria asked, snuggling her face in Tuffy's fur.

"Let's just pray it means Luther accepted Jesus as his Savior."

"Wouldn't that be wonderful?" Maria said. She hoped that was the message Luther sent.

Sammy slowed down the car. "I can't go back to Gracie's without trying one more time. Maybe if we let Tuffy out, he'll lead us to Luther. We'll follow him. I'll pull off the road and then we'll see where Tuffy goes."

After Sammy parked the car, Maria got out and set Tuffy on the ground. The dog barked and started trotting into the woods. He stopped and turned around, perhaps waiting to see if Maria and Sammy followed him. Maria ran to catch up with the dog.

"Be careful," Sammy warned, hurrying to catch her.

Is Luther under a bridge?

Maria stopped to wait for Sammy. "I think I know where he could be," she said. "We just crossed a bridge a few minutes ago. He's probably under it."

"He may be. Let's go back to the car and drive. If Luther's there *and alive*, we can get him in the car quicker." Sammy headed toward the car. Maria followed him. Tuffy turned to follow Maria. Sammy drove a short distance, and then parked the car facing the bridge. He left the headlights on.

When they walked toward the edge of the creek bank, Tuffy began to jump and bark. The closer to the bridge they got, the louder Tuffy barked. Maria felt sure Luther had taken refuge under the bridge. She climbed down the bank into the dry creek bed.

"Didn't you hear your mama? Be careful," Sammy warned, grabbing her by the arm.

How can I be careful when Luther may be dying?

Forcing her feet to walk slowly, Maria stepped into the dry creek bank. The nearer she came to the bridge, the louder her heart hammered inside her chest, and the more difficult breathing became. She decided to wait for Sammy to make the first move going under the bridge. If Luther had frozen to death, she didn't want to be the one discovering his body. Sammy stooped over to walk under the uneven wooden planks. Maria followed.

Maria took in a deep breath when she saw Luther lying on the pebble-strewn ground. His body was surrounded with dead leaves. An empty fruit jar lay nearby.

Papa was right.

She watched as Tuffy walked toward his master, licked his face, then barked, but Luther gave no response.

Is he alive?

Sammy knelt on the ground to put his finger under Luther's nostrils to feel his breath, if he were still alive. He picked up Luther's arm to feel for a pulse. After a long wait, Sammy looked up at Maria. A frown covered his face. He shook his head from side to side.

"Nothing. He's not breathing," he said.

Maria felt tears stinging her eyes, but not for Luther as much as for Gracie and Tuffy. They both loved this scoundrel. Possibly, no one else, except for the Heavenly Father loved the man. Maria felt a sob escape her lips. She pulled at Papa's coat. "Let's go," she whispered.

"There's nothing we can do," Sammy said, straightening up. "We'll have to get help."

They started back toward the car. When Maria reached down to get Tuffy, she saw a twig on the ground beside some scribbling dug into the sand. Had Luther left another message?

"Papa, come look at this," Maria said, pointing to the loose dirt. "It looks like writing. Maybe Luther left a note for Gracie."

Sammy stooped over to try to read the words. He shook his head. "I can't read it. We need to look at it in the daylight, or bring a lantern to read by."

"I sure hope it's here when we come back," Maria said. She picked up Tuffy and kept looking back as she left the creek bed. "What did Luther write, Tuffy?" she whispered.

*   *   *

Sammy and Maria saw Gracie and Louisa rushing out the door when they arrived at the house. Maria didn't know how Papa would break the news to Gracie, but he was a preacher. Delivering sad news went along with his job.

They walked into the house, took off their coats, and sat down.

"You found Tuffy!" Gracie said. The dog jumped into her lap. She fiddled with the piece of cloth tied to the leather string, but didn't look at it.

"The news is not good, Gracie," Sammy said, staring at the floor.

Gracie gasped and covered her mouth with both hands. "Oh, no!"

"Luther is dead."

"Oh, I can't believe it," Gracie said. Her face turned pale and she cried softly.

"We found Luther's body under the bridge up the road a ways. Apparently, he died from exposure to the cold."

Gracie rocked back and forth, clinging to Tuffy.

"I need to get a couple of men to help move the body from the bridge. Who do you think would be willing to do that?"

"Nearly anybody is willing to help with problems like that. Go get Boogie. Maybe there's a drunk spending the night at his house," Gracie said. She looked down at the piece of cloth. "Why, this says 'Jesus'! Wonder what that means? You think maybe he accepted the Lord before he died?"

"That's what we're praying for," Sammy answered.

"There's another message from Luther. We need to take a lantern down to the creek bed. Evidently, Luther wrote something in the sand with a stick or his finger. Do you have a lantern we can borrow?"

"A lantern? Yes. I'll go get it. Is Luther's body under the bridge just up the road?"

"Yes. It's not far from here," Sammy answered.

"Looks like he could have made it the rest of the way home," Gracie said, rising to go get the lantern. "Or, I could have walked that far, looking for him. Why didn't you come straight home with the note, Tuffy?"

When she returned with the lantern, she set it down at Sammy's feet. She walked into another room to return with her coat. "I'll go with you. I want to read Luther's last words."

Later, Gracie read the words scribbled in the sandy creek bank: "Jesus saved me. I love you, Gracie. L. D. L." Even in grief, the group praised the Lord that Luther had trusted Jesus before he died.

This is wonderful news! Is Luther L. D. L.?

Maria knew that before they left for home, she must ask Gracie about Luther's initial 'D'. She waited for a time when they were alone to inquire. "What does the D in Luther's name stand for, Gracie?" she asked, later.

"Luther Don Langley," Gracie answered in a tearful voice. *Another mystery may be solved!*

*   *   *

Gracie asked Sammy to get someone to make a pine box to hold Luther's body. Sammy bought several strips on pinewood and took them for Tobias to hammer a box together. Years before, Tobias had build his own burial box when he was condemned to death. At the last minute, his pa, Hal Johnson, had taken his place at the execution site. Tobias returned home to live a dedicated Christian life.

Maria thanked Sammy for allowing her stay out of school to attend the services. As she walked up the rock path to the house, she looked at the dead stalks covering the flower garden. *Once they were bursting with blooms.* She heard the squeaking of the garden gate and men walking on the rocks following her as they carried the pine box. She hurried to step onto the porch.

Since the weather had warmed up some, Gracie decided to hold Luther's funeral service on the front porch of their house. Only a handful of folks attended. Sammy delivered a short sermon ending triumphantly with the news that Luther had been saved before he died. Gracie sobbed as she held her two dogs, Tuffy and Teency. Gracie needed friends to comfort her. The animals served the purpose well.

Gracie had asked Sammy to take the tailgate from the cart so the wooden box would fit inside. White Lightning pulled the cart to a parcel of ground in the pasture. Tuffy sat inside guarding Luther's body while a man walked along guiding the goat to the burial spot. Gracie carried Teency. Everyone walked to the pasture behind the house. Men from the neighborhood had dug the grave. Now, they stood silently while Sammy completed the service.

When they returned to the house, Maria made a mental note: *I must visit Gracie.*

Chapter Twenty

Maria didn't know how she would tell Austin that Luther's initials were L. D. L. She didn't know *if* she would tell him.

Is this just a coincidence or is Luther really Austin's pa? I'll write to Jonathan and ask him what he would do.

Before bedtime each night, Maria stayed in the front room of the house close to the wood heater to study her lessons and write letters to Jonathan. In the next letter to Jonathan, she told about Luther's salvation. She attempted to compose the right question about Luther's initials being the same as those carved on the tree. She wrote and erased several times before writing Jonathan about the news. Finally, she just stated the simple facts.

Then her mind would go back to the question of whether or not she should buy a Christmas gift for Jonathan.

The next day after school, Maria stopped by Flodell's house hoping to get her opinion about giving Jonathan a gift. When she knocked on the door, Caleb answered.

"Is Flodell at home?" she asked.

Caleb nodded and motioned toward the bed where Flodell lay sleeping. "She sleeps most of the time," he said. "Did you want something I can get for you?"

"No. I was just gonna talk to her for a minute."

Caleb led the way into the kitchen. "Come in here to talk. Maybe she'll wake up in a few minutes."

"Who's gonna help take care of Flodell when the papoose gets here?" Maria asked.

"Mama, your Grandma Wade, said she'd come stay with us and help out," Caleb replied. "I'll be washing diapers." He laughed out loud, but quickly covered his mouth to cover the sound.

"What are you laughing about?" Flodell called from the front room.

"About me washing diapers. Maria is here," Caleb answered. He signaled for Maria to follow him.

Maria walked to stand beside the bed. "How are you feeling?"

"Not good. Bringing a baby into the world is hard work."

"Is there anything Mama or I can do to help?"

"Yeah. I'm starving to death for vinegar pie. Y'all could make one for me and bring it over," Flodell answered.

"You didn't tell me that," Caleb complained.

"You don't know how to make vinegar pie."

Caleb walked toward the kitchen. "While Maria's here, she can show me how," he said.

I won't get to ask Flodell about a Christmas gift for Jonathan.

Caleb lifted a lid from the cook stove and put in several sticks of wood while Maria told him the list of ingredients to get out.

"You need to mix together vinegar, spices, and sugar in a pot and put them on the stove to simmer. While they're heating, you can mix together the pie crust and roll it out." She told him the measurements to use. Watching Caleb's brown hands as he dumped sugar into the pan plucked a chord in her heart. *Who has hands like his?* She glanced down at her own. A wave of apprehension flew through her when she saw that Caleb's hands were a bigger stronger version of her own. And her little fingers crooked like his, too. Not to mention the way his front teeth grew. *That's unusual!*

She sneaked glimpses of Caleb's hands as he set the dough board on the table to start rolling the pie crust. *Is my family kin to Caleb's?*

She almost jumped out of her chair when Caleb spoke aloud. "Maria, what are you dreaming about? I said I'm through rolling the dough, so what do I do now?" His noisy laugh pulled her back to reality.

"Get a sharp knife and cut the dough into strips," Maria heard herself answer. She felt heat rising in her face. She turned away from Caleb. Surely he couldn't read her thoughts. "When you've cut them, then layer them in a pan and pour the vinegar mixture over them. Put them in the oven to bake. Don't let them burn."

She stood up, about to leave. "I need to go home. I didn't tell Mama I was stopping by." She walked into Flodell's room. "All Caleb needs to do is bake the pie and it'll be ready. Remind him to take it out of the oven after while."

"Don't worry. I'm hungry for that pie."

"Hope you can rest. Bye." She walked to the door to leave.

"Tell Louisa it's sure hard bringing a baby into this world," Flodell called.

A few moments later, Louisa met Maria at the door. "Did you have to stay after school?" she asked. Her furrowed brow showed her concern.

"No. I stopped by to see Flodell for a minute and she was asleep. So, I showed Caleb how to make a vinegar pie. Flodell was craving some." As she walked through the front room, she dropped her books in the chair where she sat to study. Maria rushed to her room and fell onto the bed. She needed to do some serious thinking.

That picture of Caleb over at Granny Wade's favors me a lot. I wonder if we're kin to him in some way.

Maria wrestled with the idea of asking her parents about her resemblance to Caleb, but she knew she couldn't blurt out her feelings. She'd need to come up with another way. In a way, it was kind of like Austin's problem. She *might* hold the key, but she was hesitant to tell him. Wonder if Gracie could help her?

At supper that night, Maria asked, "When's the last time you saw Gracie, Papa? Is she getting over Luther's death all right?"

"We stopped by the last time we went to Sandy Hill," Sammy answered. "She was getting along as well as could be expected, with Luther's death being so sudden."

"At the funeral, I made a promise to myself that I'd visit Gracie. The next time you go to Sandy Hill, and I'm not in school, I want to get out at her house and stay. Is that okay?"

Louisa smiled. "I think it would be a relief to Gracie, don't you Sammy?"

"Sure do. So tomorrow, you come home from school real fast and we'll take you to her house," Sammy said, and bit down on a chunk of sweet potato.

Maria could hardly sleep that night. She tried to compose different ways of approaching the subject of Luther's middle initial and any connection it might have to Austin's family background. Still undecided, she felt her eyelids closing in sleep.

Chapter Twenty-One

S ammy and Louisa walked with Maria to the door at Gracie's. Maria felt a bit of uneasiness in her stomach. If her parents stayed, how could she *really* talk to Gracie about Austin's relationship to Luther?

When Gracie opened the door, she held Teency in her arms. Maria noticed her red-rimmed eyes. Gracie had been crying. Should she stay?

Gracie managed to smile when she pulled back the door for Sammy's family to step inside. Sammy cleared his throat to speak. "We're on our way to Sandy Hill for a while. Maria wanted to visit. Is that all right with you? She can go on with us if she would bother you."

"I would like for Maria to stay," Gracie said, dabbing at the tears on her cheeks. "Maybe she can get my thoughts off the heartaches." She touched Maria's coat sleeve and placed Teency in her arms. "Both these dogs are wanting my attention. Maria can help calm them down."

Maria nodded and rubbed Teency's coat. "Is it okay, Papa? I'll play with the dogs and let Gracie rest."

Not what I planned to do, but that's all right.

Louisa picked up Tuffy. "He seems to be getting more gentle now," she said, rubbing his coat. "I guess he had to be on guard when he was around Luther."

"Are you sure Maria won't bother you?"

"No. Go on about your business. Maria will be a big help," Gracie insisted.

After her parents left, Maria plopped down on the rag rug and reached for Tuffy. "He doesn't growl at me like he used to," she commented.

"I think he knows he doesn't have to defend Luther anymore. That's the only thing I can come up with," Gracie answered. "Why don't you play with the dogs while we talk? They are so lonesome for Luther; it's pitiful. Tuffy lays around most of the time and whines."

"I'll try to entertain them while I'm here," Maria said. "Do you have a ball I can roll back and forth?"

Gracie reached into her apron pocket to pull out a chewed rubber ball. She tossed it across the room. Teency ran to get it and brought it back.

"I think this will work," Maria said, tossing the ball in the air. "Why don't you get some of your work done while I'm here?"

Gracie's eyes filled with tears. "If I do, I'll probably cry. Will that bother you?"

"It may, but that's okay. You need to cry. I read somewhere that crying helps to heal." Maria rolled the ball across the rag rug. Both dogs raced for the ball and snarled at each other. Teency bit into it first and trotted back to Maria.

"I was going through some of Luther's personal things, deciding what to throw away. If you can keep the dogs occupied, that would be a big help."

"Sure."

Gracie walked out of the room and returned with a dresser drawer. Maria tried not to stare, but she stole glances at the jumbled mess of pictures, papers, and letters filling the drawer.

"Did you save the piece of cloth that was tied on the strip around Tuffy's neck?"

"Oh, yes. I could never throw that away," Gracie answered, throwing her hands across her breast. "That's my only assurance that Luther accepted Jesus before he died."

"What about the words he wrote in the sand?"

"I treasure those, but I can't save them. The scrap of cloth is the only thing I can hold in my hands."

"You're right." Maria grabbed Tuffy in both hands, and looked into his eyes. "You're a hero."

"He sure is and he was faithful to Luther till the end," Gracie said. She sobbed for a few moments. "If only he had come home after Luther tied that scrap on the piece of leather, I may have been able to save Luther."

"I think it's best to let bygones be bygones," Maria mumbled.

Gracie dug into the dresser drawer, pulling out pictures of Luther when he was a youth. "Did you know Luther attended an Indian School?" Gracie asked, handing a picture to Maria. "That's him with some of his friends."

Maria gazed at the students' pictures arranged in a rectangle on a stiff piece of paper. Aloud, she read the names of the students at Green Briar Boarding School. "One of our special friends is the superintendent there now. His name is Brother Solomon. His wife is Watema."

Austin goes to school there.

"Did you go to the same school?"

"No. I'm not Indian. I went to school at Riverview," Gracie replied. "I met Luther while I was working in a café. He used to come in with his girlfriends—some white and some Indian."

It's getting warmer.

By now Tuffy and Teency were getting tired of chasing the ball. They curled up on the rug and went to sleep.

"The dogs are sleeping. Is there anything I can do while they're asleep?"

"Drag the chair over here and I'll tell you about these things as I go through them," Gracie said.

They looked at faded pictures of Luther standing with his family; of him as a boy; and on through his growing-up years. Maria reached for a picture and uncovered a stack of letters tied with a string. "Oh,

I didn't mean to get into your love letters," she exclaimed. She felt her face warming up. "Those are only for you. I know I wouldn't want anybody reading my love letters, when I start getting them."

If Jonathan ever writes love letters.

Gracie raised her hands in rejection. "No! They're not from me. Those were from his old girlfriends. When we married, Luther brought them stuffed in a syrup bucket with his other private papers. I told you I waited on him and his girl friends at the café. I'll probably throw the letters away. After all, I *won the prize.*" She wiped at the tears streaming down her face. She grabbed the stack of letters and walked out of the room. When Maria noticed a letter slip from the string, she ran to snatch it. She glanced at the envelope as she picked it up, intending to return it to Gracie. The scrawled name read: Lucy Lincoln.

Maria's heart jumped to her throat. What should she do with the letter? Hurriedly, she stuck it in the front of her dress, but her conscience told her she shouldn't read the letter. She pulled it from her dress, planning to give it back to Gracie. But, oh, at what a price!

Hearing Gracie's footsteps walking across the kitchen floor, Maria felt panic stricken. The answer to the question may be in her hand right this minute! Dare she throw away this golden opportunity to find out about Luther's involvement with Lucy? Seeing the doorknob turn, Maria stuck the letter under the rag rug. While they talked, she'd decide on what plan of action to take. As of now, the only fact she knew was that the letter was from Lucy Lincoln: Austin's mama.

Gracie pushed the door open and walked through. The dogs looked up when she came in, but settled back to their naps. "Well, I threw the letters away. They're part of Luther's past. He was quite a Romeo back in his younger days."

"That didn't last, did it?"

"No. When we moved here across from Boogie Estep, moonshine took over," Gracie admitted. "I have a sneaking suspicion, he already knew about the still before we married. He just didn't tell me."

"What are you going to do with White Lightning?"

"Just let him keep nibbling at the undergrowth. He's good at that," Gracie replied. She lifted the dresser drawer back into her lap and started going through more papers. When she lifted one document, it shook in her hand. "This is our marriage license. Just look at Luther's signature," she said, pointing toward it. "See how plain he signed his name? That was before moonshine got a grip on his life."

Maria steadied her hand to hold the marriage license. She felt as shaky as Gracie seemed to be. She stole a look at the date on the document. 1920! They had been married fifteen years.

Austin's sixteen.

"Yes. Luther Don Langley did have good handwriting back then," Maria said, handing the copy of the license back to Gracie.

"I'll want to keep this for my memories," Gracie said, holding it to her heart for a moment.

Maria and Gracie continued to sort through the clutter. Most of it turned out to be junk to throw away. For Maria, the most important piece lay hidden under the rag rug. Gracie rose from the chair to take another load of scraps to the trash.

Now's my chance.

Maria reached under the rug to grab the letter; picked up the dogs and walked to the door. "I'm taking the dogs out for a few minutes," she called, letting the door slam behind her. She dropped the dogs on the porch and pulled the letter from the envelope. Before she had a chance to start reading, she heard the thump of Gracie's hands pushing the door open. Maria shoved the letter back down the front of her dress. Maybe it was for the best that she didn't read the letter. She felt guilty wanting to read Luther's private mail. Gracie walked out the front door to join Maria.

"Won't be long before I plant flowers again," Gracie muttered.

"It'll be a while," Maria answered. "Come on, dogs," she called, picking up Teency and Tuffy. She knew she had to return the letter some way without letting Gracie know. Purposely, she loosed Teency, hoping she would run toward Gracie.

"You get Teency," Maria called, walking through the doorway. She ran to the drawer and slipped the letter to the bottom. Then she felt her body relax.

I did the right thing.

"Why don't you finish digging through the drawer while I play with the dogs?" Maria asked. "I'll need to leave soon." She bounced the rubber ball across the room. Teency ran after it. Tuffy didn't attempt to get the ball many times. Plainly, he missed his master.

Before long, Grace found the letter from Lucy. "Lucy Lincoln! The sheriff's sister. Sometimes, he did bring her in to eat at the café. They were sure thick." Holding it up, she sighed. "Is it better to bury my head in the sand or to face the truth?" she asked. A new flood of tears started flowing.

"Once again, I'd say, 'Let bygones be bygones,' but it's your letter. Do whatever you think is best," Maria advised.

I'd give my eyeteeth to hear what that letter says.

"I'm going to read it," Gracie said. "It may be one of the reasons Luther wanted to cover his problems by drinking." She pulled the paper from the envelope and read it aloud.

"Luther Don Langley, Why didn't you marry me? You're going to be a papa, but you'll never be allowed to see your child. You are a civet cat if there ever was one. Lucy."

Oh, no. Luther is Austin's pa. But Gracie don't know who the boy is and Austin don't know who his pa is.

Maria pretended she didn't know anything about the stinking mess.

Gracie cried a while, before she stuck the letter back in the envelope. "I should have listened to you. Maybe I should keep this for information, in case the boy wants to know who his pa is, but I wouldn't know where to look for him."

"Do you remember the time Luther drove the car out of the sand for Sheriff Lincoln? I was here on a visit."

"Seems like I remember, but he was always driving cars out of the sand for strangers. Why did you ask?"

"A boy came with us. His name is-is-Austin. He's Lucy's son," Maria said just above a whisper.

"Are you sure?" Gracie demanded. "How do you know?"

"Lucy put Austin on a bus and sent him to boarding school when he was five," Maria said. "She took off to Hollywood to be a dancer. She was good at doing the Charleston."

"I'd like to believe this is true," Gracie said. She looked at the envelope to see the date.

"Gracie, I know the story. Let me tell you about it." Maria proceeded to tell about how, when she was five, she wanted to play with Austin at the cabin. Louisa wouldn't allow her to ride in a wagon, so Maria sneaked off and caused the horses to get spoofed. Caleb's legs were mangled in the accident, resulting in amputation. Brother Solomon and Watema took Austin in to rear him. Maria made it short and sweet, covering the most important details. "Do you believe me?" Maria asked.

Gracie shook her head up and down. "I do. I don't doubt the facts. Do you think I could meet Austin?"

"Yes. I'll try to get him to come by here some day. He's wondering about his pa, too."

Tuffy started barking. Maria looked out the window to see Sammy walking up the path. "I guess that means I need to leave. Will you be all right?"

"Of course. Thanks for telling me about the boy. Come another time and play with the dogs," Gracie said. "You can tell me more about Austin."

Maria walked out the door thanking the Lord she didn't read the letter. Now she knew the facts about Austin's pa without sneaking to find out. Gracie told her the truth.

Chapter Twenty-Two

*M*aria felt like White Rabbit must feel when she gathered the baby chicks into her apron. One chick always jumped out. The secrets the letter revealed kept trying to escape from her mouth. Did she want to tell her parents? Did she want to tell Austin? She *did* want to tell Jonathan.

"What did y'all do?" Louisa asked.

"Mostly I played with Teency and Tuffy while Gracie looked through a dresser drawer of Luther's personal belongings," Maria answered.

"Like what?" Sammy asked.

"Pictures of him and his family. Papers, like his and Gracie's marriage license—that kind of stuff. My job was to keep Tuffy and Teency out of Gracie's way so she could work without them pestering her," Maria answered. "Gracie wants me to come back. She thinks Tuffy is suffering from the loss of his master."

"You should go again," Louisa said.

"I'll come with you the next time you're going when I'm not in school," Maria said.

I can't wait to go back.

As soon as the supper dishes were washed, Maria headed to the chair in the corner where she sat to study and to write a letter. She laid the schoolwork aside. She needed to write Jonathan. What about Austin? Maybe she should ask Jonathan and wait for his advice.

The next morning, Maria left early for school, planning to stop at the post office to mail Jonathan's letter.

Hurry, Jonathan answer my letter. Or come see me at Christmas.

*   *   *

A few days before Christmas, Sammy sat in the front room studying for a sermon. Grandpa Tobias Grant had asked him to preach. Maria looked up from her spot in the corner to see Sammy fidgeting around, with an expression of frustration on his face.

"What's wrong, Papa?" she asked.

"Oh, I can't read the words. I need a lamp bright enough so I can see what I'm doing," Sammy complained.

"Why don't you come sit at the kitchen table?" Louisa called. "The light is brighter in here."

Sammy rose from the chair and walked into the kitchen. "Anything will be better than the light in the front room."

How about getting a lamp for Jonathan? He studies a lot. Papa needs one, too.

When Maria found Louisa alone, she suggested they combine their money to buy a brighter lamp for Sammy. With Louisa's approval, Maria went to the furniture store to look at lamps. It took all the money, but she managed to buy a lamp for both the important men in her life. She didn't know how she'd get the lamp to Jonathan by Christmas, but she felt the door would be open, someway.

Will I see Jonathan on Christmas?

Everyone got up early the morning of Christmas Eve. Louisa had some last minute baking to do. Maria rushed around helping her mama. Around ten that morning, a loud knock sounded at the door. Maria wiped her hands on a cup towel and went to answer the door. Brother Solomon, Watema, and Austin stood waiting, bundled in coats and caps.

"What a surprise!" Maria exclaimed. "Come in, before you freeze." She turned to call to Louisa, "Mama, we have company."

Everyone stood around taking off wraps; all were trying to talk at the same time. After a while, Mama took Watema into the kitchen; Papa and Brother Solomon sat in a corner of the front room; and Maria led Austin to her bedroom.

"Drag a chair in from the kitchen. What are y'all doing in Riverview?" Maria asked, plopping down on her bed.

"Watema and Brother Solomon wanted to visit Caleb," Austin said, sitting down in the ladder back chair. "They're going to stay in a tourist court tonight. I'm going to see if I can stay with Uncle Lucky. We're gonna be here tomorrow, too. What are y'all going to do tomorrow?"

"Have Christmas dinner. Don't know of much else." Did she dare ask Austin if he'd seen Jonathan? "I-uh-was hoping I could see Jonathan sometime during Christmas. Have you seen him?"

"Yes. I saw him not long ago," he answered, spreading wide his hands and staring at them. "He was asking about you, but I didn't know any news to tell him."

"We're writing to each other," Maria confided. "If he can keep his grades up, he'll have a life time teaching certificate at the end of the semester. He's going to try to get a job in one of the schools around here."

"So you can get . . .?" Austin asked, smiling.

"Get what?"

Not what I'm hoping, I'm sure.

"You know," he replied. "Get hitched."

Maria felt heat flowing through her body. Yes, she'd like to get married, but why would Austin say that? Did Jonathan confide in him?

"Maria," Louisa called. "Come help with the cooking. We'll have a Christmas Eve meal for everyone."

Maria jumped from the bed and whispered to Austin, "Don't say anything to anybody about what we were talking about."

While she picked up sticks of wood out of the wood box, Maria suddenly thought of Gracie. Wouldn't today be a perfect time for Gracie to meet Austin? "Mama!" she exclaimed.

Louisa dropped the potato she was peeling. "What on earth is wrong?" she asked.

"I just thought about Gracie staying at her house alone at Christmas. Why can't Papa go get her so she can eat with us? She needs company."

"That's a kind thought, but you didn't need to scream. That potato rolled under the ice box and I can't reach it," Louisa complained.

"I'll get it. Don't worry," Maria said, walking to get the broom. She stuck the broom handle under the icebox and raked out the potato. "You want to use it or throw it away?"

"Put it in a bowl and if I need it, I'll scrub it real good. Lower your voice, girl."

Maria walked into the front room. "Papa, why don't y'all go to Gracie's and bring her over to eat?"

Sammy stared at her with a frustrated look on his face. "Maria, you're always coming up with something for us to do."

"But she's lonely," Maria objected.

"If it's okay with your mama, I'll go," Sammy answered.

"She said it's okay."

The men left to bring Gracie over. Mama sent Maria out to the chicken pen to catch a fryer. "I'll get the water boiling to scald the feathers."

For this special occasion, Maria didn't protest over going to the hen house and grabbing a fryer by the legs. She went to the kitchen door to yell for Mama to come wring its head off, though.

Out on the back porch, after dipping the chicken in hot water, Mama made short work of plucking the feathers. Hurriedly, she took the bare fowl into the house. Inside, she plunged the chicken into another pot of hot water to loosen the pinfeathers. "We'll have fried chicken and gravy and mashed potatoes. I'll bake a pan of hot biscuits, too," Louisa said. "Does that sound all right, Watema?"

"Real good," Watema agreed. "You don't have to cook for us. We can go to the café to eat."

"Seems I heard that before," Louisa said, then she laughed. "I'm saving the food I've already cooked for tomorrow, but we'll have plenty for dinner today. Maria, put on a pot of coffee."

The next several minutes Louisa spent getting all the pinfeathers off the fryer and cutting it up for frying. Soon, she floured the pieces and put them into a skillet of hot lard to fry. "I'm through with the biggest job. Watema, why don't you watch the chicken while Maria and I fix the other food? I'll get you an apron."

While the women talked, Maria wondered how to bring up the subject of Luther's relationship to Austin. Just blurt it out or ease into it?

*   *   *

"I've been here before," Austin said, when Sammy pulled the car beside the fence. "We brought Flodell out to get her clothes the day she left home. Uncle Lucky got stuck in the sand and a man who lived in this house had to drive the car out."

"I was put out with Maria for riding out here to get Flodell, but at least y'all are safe," Sammy said, getting out of the car. "I'll be back in a minute."

"What happened?" Brother Solomon asked, looking over his shoulder at Austin.

"Maria and I were trying to save money on the tickets, so we rode with Eli. We met Flodell when Eli drove out here to see her. Flodell's parents live over that way," Austin said, pointing toward Boogie's house. "The next day, Flodell's pa threw her out."

"I'm glad Caleb married her," Brother Solomon said. "At least, she's happier now than before."

Austin looked up to see Gracie, somewhat flustered, walking down the rock pathway. Two dogs peeked from the front of Gracie's coat. Sammy helped her get in the backseat with Austin.

"You know Austin, don't you?" Sammy asked, starting up the engine.

"Austin? Oh, yes I saw him when he came here with Sheriff Lincoln," Gracie said. She reached across the seat in front of her to tap Sammy on the shoulder. "I sure hate to ask you to wait for me, but I left an important paper in the house. I'll run get it—won't take but a minute." She pushed the dogs into Austin's lap.

While she hurried back to the house, Sammy laughed and said, "That's the way with women, Austin. Get ready to sit and wait when you decide to get married."

Austin felt his face heating up. *I'm not thinking about marriage.*

When Gracie crawled into the backseat, she extended her right hand to Austin to shake his. "Glad to meet you. I'm Gracie." She took Teency from Austin's lap. "You can hold Tuffy, my dead husband's dog."

"Your *dead* husband! You mean the man who drove the car out of the sand bed is dead?"

Austin looked at Tuffy. He seemed calmer than when Luther carried him down the road back in the summer.

Gracie nodded. "Yes," she said. She stared at Austin for a long time.

Austin wanted to shrink into a ball to keep this strange woman from scrutinizing him so closely. He put his hand to his mouth, pretending to cough.

"Are we ready to go?" Sammy interrupted.

"Let's go. Dinner may be ready by the time we get back," Brother Solomon said.

"Do you remember the man who drove Sheriff Lincoln's car out of the sand?" Gracie asked, quietly.

"A little bit," Austin admitted.

"His name was Luther Don Langley," Gracie pronounced each word distinctly. "He died not long ago. Froze to death under a bridge back down the road."

Austin stopped listening when Gracie said the words: "Luther Don Langley."

L. D. L. He couldn't be my pa. Not that drunk Indian.

"I'm sorry," Austin mumbled.

"We all are," Gracie said. She reached over to pet Tuffy. "Especially Tuffy. He's cried and whined most of the time since Luther's death, but he's behaving better now. Doesn't get angry and snap at people like he used to."

"Yeah. I remember the first time I saw Tuffy. He bit at me like he was about to take a chunk out of my hand," Austin said.

L. D. L. Tuffy. It can't be. I've got to look at the tree while we're here.

Austin coughed again and cleared his throat. "Sammy," he said. "I don't know when I'll be back again, so would you stop so I can see that carved heart one more time?"

"What for?" Brother Solomon asked. Austin knew the preacher was irritated with the request. During this cold spell was not a good time to be looking at a heart carved on a tree.

"Please. It can be my Christmas present," Austin pleaded.

"I'll remember that," Brother Solomon said.

"Does this have anything to do with Luther?" Gracie asked.

"It might," Sammy said, pulling the car near the trees. Austin handed Tuffy to Gracie before he and Sammy climbed out to hurry over to the tree. Sammy kicked several empty fruit jars away from the tree. "This is disgusting," he said.

Austin rubbed his fingers over the initials "L. D. L." and showed them to Sammy.

"What do you think?" he asked.

"Any thing is possible," Sammy said. "Maybe we can pin down your uncle while you're here and get his opinion. How about that?" He looked at Austin for affirmation.

"I'd like that. I'm ready. Let's go," Austin said, rubbing his fingers over both sets of initials one last time.

When Austin turned from the tree, he bumped into Gracie. She had followed them. He noticed she was wiping tears from her eyes.

The conversation about Luther Don Langley was dropped, once

they were on their way to Riverview. Everyone was lost in his own thoughts, especially Austin.

"Oh, I forgot. We have a surprise for Maria tonight," Brother Solomon said. "Jonathan is in town. He came with us to visit Maria."

Sammy exhaled a long sigh.

"Won't she be tickled to death?" Gracie asked. "The last time she was at my house, I could tell she was love sick."

"She'll be thrilled to death, I'm sure. She may be the only one," Sammy said. He pushed down on the foot feed when he turned off on the main road.

"This Christmas season may open the eyes of several people," Austin mused.

Especially mine.

Chapter Twenty-Three

*E*veryone sat around the kitchen table enjoying the meal. Except for Austin. He pretended to eat but the news about Luther Don Langley kept interfering with his appetite. Was Gracie's deceased husband his father? Maybe being kept in the dark was a blessing. The report about Austin's relationship to Luther beat in his brain like a drum in the marching band at Green Briar. Nothing he could do would change his parentage. Just as well relax and enjoy the meal.

When everyone finished eating, women started clearing the table. The men went into the front room to talk.

"Could we save these chicken bones for my dogs?" Gracie asked, as she scraped the leftovers from the plates. "They like to gnaw on bones."

"What dog doesn't?" asked Maria, pretending to toss a bone in the air.

"Don't you dare to throw a chicken bone in this kitchen," Louisa said, swatting at Maria with a cup towel. "Tomorrow's Christmas Day, remember? The kitchen needs to be clean for the big meal.

"We'll wash the dishes and then everyone can sit back and enjoy another cup of coffee."

"Yes, that would be nice. And while we're all together, I have a question to ask," Gracie said.

What about? Austin wondered. *She's already said too much.*

In a few moments, while everyone sipped his coffee, Gracie said,

"Since I've been going to the meetings at Sandy Hill, Sammy quoted a Bible verse for me. It's found in Romans 8:28. Luther just died in a horrible way. I need to know how all things work together for good in that situation."

Austin watched Sammy reach for a Bible. Brother Solomon felt in his coat pocket. Both men appeared apprehensive.

"Like I said before, we need to remember the words, 'love God'. If we don't love God, then the verse doesn't apply to us," Sammy said. "Do you agree, Brother Solomon?"

"Yes, and the other important words are 'the called according to *his* purpose'," said Brother Solomon. "I, personally, believe not everyone can claim that promise, though most Christians do when they're in trouble."

"The last time I tried to explain the verse, I used Joseph enduring lots of problems. Finally the trials ended with Joseph's family being reunited. Now I'll go a different direction." He turned to Louisa and asked, "How did you make the vinegar pie?"

"Why?" Louisa asked. "Are you getting a sick stomach?"

"No," Sammy said, and then he laughed. "Just tell me one ingredient."

"Vinegar."

"Does vinegar have a good taste?"

"No, but—"

"Another ingredient, please."

"Flour."

"Just imagine," Sammy said, "the cook dumping a cupful of flour in your plate. Would that taste good?"

"Horrible. But where are you going with the vinegar pie talk?" Maria asked.

Sammy smiled at Maria. "Just hold your horses. More ingredients, Louisa."

"Lard, salt, spices, sugar, even water," Louisa counted off on her fingers.

"None of those taste good alone, except sugar and water. You sure don't want to eat pure sugar. Are you getting the idea, Gracie?"

" I *think* so, but go ahead," Gracie answered, rubbing her brow.

"Which of those ingredients are put into the pie crust?"

"Flour, lard, salt, and water," Louisa answered.

"All those ingredients make a crispy pie crust when mixed together and baked, but please don't set a bucket of lard on the table for a meal."

"Yuck," Watema exclaimed. "Is this helping you, Gracie?"

"Yes, I see it!" Gracie exclaimed. "All the things that happen may be bad when they come one at a time, but put them all together and something good comes out. To those who love God and are the called according to His purpose, of course. Thank you, Sammy."

"Yeah, Papa, that made it clear even to me," Maria said.

"It helps me, too," Austin commented.

Maybe someday I'll see how all my problems come out to the glory of God.

"Now I can look for the good to come from all those things I've been through, if I am living in accordance with God's commands," Gracie said. She smiled through a flood of tears.

When the tears stopped flowing and the conversation turned to a lighter topic, Austin and Maria slipped back into Maria's bedroom to discuss subjects young people liked to talk about—fellers and girlfriends. In a minute, Gracie came into the room carrying her purse. She closed the door quietly.

"Austin," she said just above a whisper, "I have a letter I want to give to you."

Austin felt his body tense up.

What's she talking about?

"From now on, you won't need to worry about the question of who your papa was. It's right here in black and white."

Austin felt like an arrow had pierced his heart. And it would injure him if he pulled it out. Did he just sit and listen to Gracie's disclosure or bolt and run? He'd wanted to learn about his real father ever since he was big enough to understand. He decided to sit and let the arrow sink in even deeper.

Gracie pulled the yellowed letter from her purse. "When I realized you were in the car, I went back into the house to get the letter. You can have it. It verifies that Luther Don Langley was your father." She thrust the letter into Austin's hands.

Austin felt as if he held live coals when he accepted the letter. It trembled in his hands.

What would Luther's son do? Accept the letter in a kind manner? Tear it to shreds? Stomp on it? Throw it in the fire?

"Thanks, Gracie," he stammered. He walked over to stand near the window and read the stinging words his mama had written to Luther. So Luther was his papa! Carefully, he folded the paper and inserted it into the envelope. He stuck it in his shirt pocket. He would decide what to do with it later. "I guess I've got a bellyful for now. I need to go stay all night with Uncle Lucky. Probably won't sleep a wink."

He extended his right hand and shook Gracie's. "Thanks," he repeated. "I'll be around tomorrow, I reckon."

Soon, he and Brother Solomon walked out the door. No one saw the arrow sticking from Austin's heart, but he felt it piercing all the way through.

*   *   *

Maria stayed in her room for a few minutes, trying to calm herself down. She already knew about Luther and Lucy's affair, so she felt no shock; only empathy for Austin.

A lot of times I wonder about my life.

Shaking off the bewilderment that engulfed her, she walked into the front room to listen to the conversation. She picked up Teency and smoothed her coat. She could feel Teency relaxing and knew she would soon fall asleep. In a few minutes, a knock sounded at the door. "Come on in, Brother Solomon," Sammy called.

"He didn't need to knock," Louisa said.

Maria watched the doorknob turn, expecting Brother Solomon to walk in, but a tall young Indian man stepped inside first. Maria's heart jumped into her throat. The man was a dead ringer for Jonathan . . . like his identical twin.

"It's sure cold –," he began.

Jonathan's voice.

Maria jumped from the chair, letting Teency fall to the floor. "Jonathan, is that you?" she asked loudly.

"Sure is," Jonathan answered, coming to take her by the hands. "I came to see you for Christmas. Are you surprised?"

Maria nodded her head up and down. "I think I'm going to faint. Or else I'm dreaming."

Jonathan pulled a chair beside her, and sat gazing into her eyes and holding her hands. "No, you're not dreaming. I'm really here." He gave her hands a squeeze.

Thank you, Dear Jesus. Jonathan came to visit me.

"I'm sure glad," Maria managed to say, gazing into his black eyes.

"Perhaps Jonathan would like a bite to eat," Louisa suggested. "Take him into the kitchen and give him some of the leftovers."

"No, no, I'm not hungry," protested Jonathan.

Maria pulled him from the chair and directed him toward the kitchen. "Yes, you are," she mouthed. She showed him a place to sit while she got a clean plate from the cabinet. "We've got a few pieces of fried chicken, mashed potatoes, gravy and some biscuits. How does that sound?" She opened a drawer to pull out a knife, fork, and spoon.

"Sounds good. Give me small helpings," Jonathan said, smiling at her. "I'm not really hungry, but I'm glad to be in here with you," he whispered.

"Pretend you're hungry," Maria whispered back.

While Jonathan ate small bites of the mashed potatoes and gravy, he explained that he wanted to surprise her. He got in touch with Brother Solomon, who made arrangements to bring him to Riverview.

"How are your classes going at college?" Maria asked. "You think you'll get your life teaching certificate?" She held her breath, hoping he'd answer 'yes'.

Jonathan shook his head up and down as he swallowed a bite of biscuit. "I'm going to make it. I'll be through by the middle of January. And then . . . "

"Then what?" Maria demanded.

"We can see each other more often," Jonathan answered, touching her hand.

That's less than a month away.

"I'm sure glad. Did you get my letter about Austin?"

Jonathan nodded. "I've been praying about how to answer."

"Well, the Lord answered your prayer. Austin found out who his papa was. Gracie gave him a letter Lucy Lincoln wrote to Luther before Austin was born. So now he knows."

"I guess he'll tell me about it later. I suppose he's relieved."

"I don't know, but he'll be here to eat Christmas dinner tomorrow," Maria answered. "We can see how he acts then."

Jonathan finished his food and stood. "I need to be polite and visit with the other folks."

Maria felt a cold wave of disappointment sweep over her. She couldn't hogtie Jonathan in the chair at the table, so she forced herself to smile and agreed.

"Maybe I can borrow Brother Solomon's car and we can go for a drive tomorrow. I want to have some time alone with you while I'm here."

"That sounds good."

They walked into the front room to visit with the older folks. Maria couldn't concentrate on what they said, because she focused only on Jonathan. Much too soon for her, Brother Solomon stood, and motioned for Watema to get their coats.

"We need to be leaving," Brother Solomon said. "Tomorrow we'll be back. It's possible Austin will be with us, and for sure, Jonathan will come." He smiled at Maria and winked.

Maria's arms itched to give Jonathan a bear hug, but she'd have to wait till they were alone tomorrow. She stood on the porch watching the car, till it drove out of sight.

What dress will I wear tomorrow? Tomorrow . . .

Chapter Twenty-Four

*M*aria got up early to choose the prettiest dress she owned. For five cents, she'd walk to Flodell's to borrow her beautiful wedding dress.

But Jonathan saw it at the wedding. He might think I'm hinting at marriage.

She decided to wear her red dress and tie red ribbons in her hair. She'd put those on at the last minute. Now, she must help Mama and Gracie with the details of preparing the big Christmas dinner. The meal wasn't ready when several members of the Grant family began arriving. Sammy's sister, Hallie, with her husband Junior Maytubby, got there first. Junior wanted to visit with his mama, Watema.

Granny Wade came in with White Rabbit and Tobias. Maria looked up to see Brother Solomon, Watema, and Austin walk in soon after. She ran to her room to put on her red dress before Jonathan saw her. When she walked out, Jonathan headed straight for her and grabbed her hand.

To accommodate the crowd, Sammy laid flat boards across chairs and Louisa had covered them with tablecloths to furnish more eating space. The makeshift table had been set up in the front room. Grandpa Tobias Grant led in prayer before everyone began passing around the bowls of food. White Rabbit had brought a huge pot filled with chicken and dumplings. Granny Wade added a roaster full of baked sweet potatoes. Hallie's contribution was a dish of *tafula*, (hominy). Louisa prepared big pots of *pishofa*, (hominy with pork) mashed potatoes, *tanchi puluska* (corn bread) and *tobi* (beans). For dessert, she cooked up a pot of grape dumplings and baked vinegar pies.

"If I had known before hand, I would have brought some food," Gracie said, apologetically.

"You brought yourself and your dogs," Louisa said. "That's enough.

"Maria, why don't you put back some food for Flodell and Caleb?" Louisa asked. "I know Flodell doesn't feel like cooking and Caleb is just learning how."

"I'll do that," Watema said. "Caleb is my son and Flodell is my daughter-in-law. It's the least I can do." She dropped her fork and reached for two plates to fill. She covered them with cup towels so they'd stay warm.

After everyone finished eating, the women cleaned up the kitchen. Brother Solomon left with Watema, Hallie, and Junior for Caleb's to deliver the plates of food. Sammy loaded up the others in his car and followed.

Maria watched Flodell's eyes light up when the visitors entered the house. "Company on Christmas! Isn't that nice?" Flodell said. Maria noticed Flodell's blonde hair hadn't been combed and the back of it was matted and tangled. Her face was pale and colorless.

She must feel bad. She's not wearing her lipstick.

When she saw the food, Flodell added, "Oh, good. Christmas dinner, too. I smell the vinegar pie. Yum, yum. Caleb's in the kitchen, trying to cook.

"Caleb," she called. "Stop cooking. Your mama brought dinner over."

While she ate, Flodell asked about how to cook the *pishofa*. "You listen to Louisa, Caleb."

"It's made out of *tafula*, mixed with pork," Louisa said.

"What's *tafula*?" Flodell asked.

"Hominy," Caleb answered.

Everyone visited for a while, but Maria sensed most folks were uncomfortable being around Flodell. She barely picked at her food and she seemed jittery. They said their good-byes and went back to Louisa's.

Back at the house, Maria wondered about giving the Christmas gift to Jonathan. She motioned for him to come to her room. She didn't want the others to see her giving Jonathan his gift. Shyly, she reached under her bed and brought out the lamp. "It's for you to study by," she said, pulling off the wrapping paper.

"That is so nice of you. I can sure use it," Jonathan said. Glancing at the closed door, he gave her a quick hug. "Thanks," he whispered. "Ready to go for that ride?"

That was worth every penny the lamp cost.

Maria decided that Jonathan must have prearranged with Brother Solomon to use his car, because he didn't need to ask. They pulled on their coats and started out the door.

"Maria," Louisa called. "Why don't y'all drive by Flodell's before you come back? I didn't like the way she looked while ago."

"We'll do that," Jonathan said.

Inside the car, Maria snuggled close to Jonathan. He slipped his free arm around her. "Thanks for the lamp. I have lots of last minute studying and then the final exams. I'll use it every night till school's out."

"I thought you could use it when you're preparing sermons, too," Maria said.

"I sure will. I'm supposed to preach at Tobias' church Sunday. Will you be there?"

"Wild horses couldn't keep me away," Maria said. *I shouldn't have said that.* "But you know sickness or a bad accident could," she added quickly.

"Let's drive to the church and look around," Jonathan suggested.

"Fine. You can practice on me, preaching the sermon."

Jonathan drove to the church and parked. He and Maria got out and ran inside the building. Jonathan kicked the door closed and grabbed Maria in his arms. "I love you, Maria. I love you very much," he said, swinging her around.

Maria's heart melted like warm chocolate. She'd waited to hear those words since summer. "I love you, too," she answered.

"I fell in love with you that day when you said you were the Prodigal Daughter. May I prove it with a kiss?"

"Uh huh," Maria answered.

Hurry or I'm gonna pass out.

Together they shared their first romantic kiss. Maria's heart beat all kinds of love songs while Jonathan wrapped her in his arms. In her wildest dreams, she hadn't imagined love would be so satisfying as this.

"Oh, Jonathan. You're just perfect for me," she whispered.

"And you are for me," Jonathan said.

They sat on a bench and gazed into each other's eyes for a few moments.

Jonathan is so good to me—and kind—and handsome. I can't believe he loves me.

"You're sure pretty in that red dress with the ribbons in your hair. You're so much nicer than the girls I've met at the college," Jonathan said, squeezing her hand. "I found myself comparing you with those girls and you came out winner every time."

"Thanks. If I compared you with Orville, there wouldn't be a contest. You'd win, hands down," Maria said. "In fact, I noticed that while we were on the train. Even at the beginning I was glad Orville didn't love me. The Lord took care of me."

"And saved you for me?" Jonathan asked. "He sure did." He glanced out the window. "How long does it take to make a wedding dress?"

Maria almost fell off the bench. Did Jonathan mention *wedding dress?* "For who?" she asked, pretending she didn't know.

"For you." He got down on one knee. "Maria, I'm asking you to marry me. As soon as my classes are over, I want to come back and we can get married."

"Oh, I can't believe it! I'm sure I can get a dress ready by the middle of January."

"Then the answer is yes?"

"Yes, a thousand times yes," Maria answered.

"Then look out the window. It's snowing. Isn't it a special time with snow falling, when . . . " Sticking his hand into his pocket, he pulled out a small box. "I present you with your Christmas present? It may not fit, though." He opened a box to reveal a gold band. "It's for you to wear at our wedding. Try it on." He rose from his knees.

Maria dropped the ring before she could get it on. Jonathan leaned over to pick it up. Finally, he helped her get the ring on the right finger.

"It fits fine," Maria said, putting her hand over her heart. "It feels so good, I don't want to take it off."

"Oh, but you have to. I need to finish my classes before we get married," Jonathan said. "Let's go back and tell everybody that we're engaged." They shared another lingering kiss, sealing the commitment.

When they were in the car, Maria asked Jonathan to drive by Doc Coleman's office. "Just in case Flodell's baby is born today. Wouldn't it be a good time for the baby to come on Christmas and while it's snowing?"

"Yes!" Jonathan said. He drove by Doc Coleman's office and got out. When he returned, his brow was creased with worry lines. "A sign on the door says Doc Coleman's office is closed for Christmas."

"Papa can be the doctor if he has to," Maria said. "Now, we need to go see about Flodell."

When they walked inside, Flodell was eating again. She had a fork loaded with *pishofa,* ready to take a big bite when suddenly she dropped it and bit her lips. She covered her mouth with both hands, keeping them there for a long time.

Maria hurried toward her. "What's wrong?" she asked. "Is the *pishofa* that bad?"

"I didn't taste it," Flodell answered, weakly. "I just had a horrible pain. It hurt bad."

Oh, boy! Maybe her time has come.

In a few minutes, Flodell started to eat again. "I'm okay," she said. "False alarm. One of these days it won't be a false alarm, though. Who around here knows anything about birthing babies?"

"Papa does," Maria answered. "He helped Doc Coleman birth babies before he went off to college." She glanced at Jonathan. "We'd better go. I'll tell Papa he needs to come see about you after while."

They drove to the house to tell Sammy he might be needed soon. Most of the relatives had left when the snow started falling. Only Gracie, Brother Solomon, and Watema remained.

"It's too bad everybody left before they heard the big news," Maria said. "It looks like Flodell's time has come."

"Wouldn't a Christmas baby be wonderful?" Louisa asked. "Only thing, Doc is probably not in his office." She sent a knowing glance toward Sammy. "You know what that means."

"I hope not," Sammy said, heaving a sigh. "You're right, Doc's office is closed today."

"Most of the time it takes quite a while for a baby to be born," Sammy said. "I'll go over in about an hour, but I think that's too soon."

When no one was looking, Maria grabbed Mama's arm and pulled her into her room. "Jonathan asked me to marry him," Maria whispered. "He gave me a wedding band."

Mama smiled and hugged Maria.

"Don't tell anybody yet. Wait till Flodell's baby is born. She's got the important news for today."

Soon, Sammy, Louisa, Jonathan, and Maria loaded into Sammy's car to go to Flodell's house. Watema and Gracie rode in the car with Brother Solomon.

When she walked into the front room at Caleb's, Maria heard Flodell crying out in pain. The moans tore at Maria's heart. She watched Flodell reach for the iron rails at the head of the bed and hold so tightly her knuckles stuck out.

Sammy pushed Maria out of the way and grabbed Flodell's hand. "Stop pushing," he said. Turning to Caleb he said, "It's getting close to time. If you want me to, Louisa and I will take over. Doc's office is closed. Gracie, we may need you."

"Take over," Caleb said. He grabbed Maria's arm and led her into the kitchen.

The others followed them into the kitchen. Sammy motioned for Caleb to pour hot water into the washbasin. They scrubbed their hands thoroughly and returned to the front room. "I could sure use more light," Sammy said.

Papa's Christmas present.

Maria whispered to Jonathan. "Can you take me home to get the lamp I bought for Papa? It's just like yours."

"Sure. Let's go." He walked by Brother Solomon to tell him he needed the car for a few minutes.

Soon they returned with the lamp. Louisa took it into the front room and set it on a table near the bed. She plugged it into the electrical outlet.

"That's much better. I think I can see now."

Maria heard Sammy speaking to Flodell. "When I tell you to push; push with all your might, but if I say stop, you stop."

"Are you scared?" Maria asked Caleb.

"Yeah. She's been hurting something awful. I'm worried about her."

"I know. She hasn't been looking good for a long time. Maybe I should make a pot of coffee for everybody in case there's a long wait."

Caleb pointed to the coffee pot, the coffee, and the water. "I hope it don't take too much longer. I'm tired out already."

"Yeah, but think about poor Flodell," Watema said.

"Forget about yourself," Maria said, dumping coffee granules into the pot and filling it with water. She set the pot on to brew.

A loud moan came from the front room. It sent chills over Maria's body.

I might not be able to stand this.

Caleb walked to the door and peeked through a crack. "She looks awful," he said.

After a while, Gracie slipped into the kitchen, followed by Sammy. Gracie asked, "Did Flodell get any blankets to wrap the baby in? We'll need some. If you don't have any, get a sheet or another piece of cloth."

"Yeah," Sammy said. "Even a shirt will do. That's what Maria was wrapped in when she was born." He laughed nervously.

Mama didn't even get a blanket for me?

Caleb stared at Maria with a look of admiration on his face. "My daughter— wearing a shirt when she was just born?"

"Your daughter!" Maria exclaimed. "You're not thinking straight. Flodell's pain is getting the best of you."

Jonathan walked to stand beside Maria. "Just hold your horses," he whispered. "He's mixed up."

What is Caleb talking about?

Sammy looked at Caleb and nodded up and down. "He's right," Sammy said. "Go ahead, Caleb. Tell her the truth. Gracie, you go stay with Flodell and send Louisa back in here."

Louisa walked in. She took Maria's hand and asked, "Remember when Granny Wade told Flodell about the girl living in the cabin?"

Maria nodded.

But I'm not part of that story—am I?

"I was the girl who went to live in the cabin," Mama said, rubbing Maria's shoulder.

"What?" Maria screamed, forgetting all about Flodell in the other room. She jumped from the chair and clamped her hands on her hips. "You were not and I'm not going to listen to this." She started for the backdoor.

Louisa grabbed hold of her dress, to pull her back. "Maria, you were born in the cabin," she whispered. "Hallie and Sammy are the ones who birthed you."

"I don't want to hear this," Maria said, covering her ears with her hands.

"It's time you learned the truth," Caleb said. "I'm your pa. Watema and Brother Solomon are your grandparents. Just like Granny Wade is."

Maria fell back into her chair and covered her face with her hands. "Is that all or is another piece of the sky gonna fall?"

"Maria, just listen to them," Jonathan said, grabbing her by the hand.

"It's not as terrible as it sounds," Louisa began.

"No, it's worse than it sounds," Maria said. "How could it get—?"

"It's not your mama's fault," Caleb interrupted, touching her gently. "I'm the one to blame. The total blame falls on me. I forced Louisa into it."

"And because my papa was a preacher, I went to live in the cabin to keep from disgracing him," Louisa added. "While Hallie was visiting me, Sammy and Toby were out looking for her and that's where I met them—at the cabin." When Maria saw Louisa's lips quivering, she knew Mama was fighting for composure.

"At first, I thought about giving you away to Hallie and Junior, but I couldn't. I loved you too much."

"I acted like I knew nothing about the whole escapade," Caleb said. "I played dumb for a long time and let her go on bearing all the blame. After years of acting cruel and hateful, I saw I was treating your mama like Jesus was treated when He was hanging on the cross. He bore the sins of ever body who will ever live. Your mama was bearing both our sins all by herself, all alone. I asked for forgiveness. By then you were a big girl." He held out his hand to show her height.

Now's the time to get some things straight.

Maria grabbed Caleb's hand and put hers beside it. "Are they shaped alike? Are my little fingers crooked like yours?"

Jonathan examined their hands and nodded. "The same exactly."

"I noticed the resemblance not long ago. And our teeth are alike, too."

"Like father, like daughter," Caleb said, and smiled.

Maria turned to her mama. "So Grandpa Wade never made things right with you till the night he died?" she asked.

"That's it exactly. I loved Papa, but he let pride ruin his life," Louisa said. "He was too proud to acknowledge that one of his daughters could turn out like I did. I tried to explain, and Mama tried to help, but he wouldn't listen to anybody's explanation. He took his spite out on everybody in the family."

"Your mother went through torture to protect the family name," Sammy said. "She deserves a medal for valor." He took Louisa by the hand and kissed it.

Sammy looked at Maria. "It's true, the first blanket you wore was my shirt."

"What? A tiny baby wearing a man's shirt?" Maria exclaimed.

"Yes, right after your birth, Hallie asked me to take off my shirt and wrap you in it," Sammy said. "Your mama got her first look at you wearing my shirt."

"I'll bet that's a record. Most babies are wrapped in blankets," Jonathan said. He turned to Caleb. "Caleb, Flodell probably has plenty of blankets, but I have an idea. Just as a family tradition, why don't you go get one of your shirts to wrap the new baby in?"

Caleb nodded and left the room.

"Well, Maria you're different in a lot of ways," Louisa said. She smiled at her daughter. "You entered this world in an original place—a deserted cabin—and you've been unique all your life. Headstrong, for one thing."

"Yeah, I'm different. I have two papas and two mamas," Maria exclaimed.

And one husband-to-be. And I was proposed to in the middle of a snowstorm.

"Do you understand it all now?" Louisa asked. "Nothing will be changed, except that a new baby is added to the family."

I can't believe Caleb is my real papa.

"Yeah. I'll try to straighten it all out as time goes by. But it still hurts."

"Maybe we should have waited till the baby got here," Caleb said, walking back into the room, "but I wanted Flodell to know she is your stepmother."

"You could have told her and left me in the dark," Maria said, "but now that it's out in the open, a big question in my life has been answered."

"You're my daughter," Sammy emphasized. "You have been since you were just born. Hallie and I were the first two people to see you, even before Louisa did. Toby was the next one after Louisa. So, you've been mine from the day you were born."

So that's the family secret. I can't believe Caleb is my real papa.

Caleb walked to shake hands with Sammy. "You took my place. Thanks, Brother."

"I brought two shirts," he said, holding them up. "Which one should we use, Maria?"

Maria took the first shirt she touched. It didn't matter. She turned out all right, wrapped in a man's shirt.

At that moment, Gracie yelled, "Sammy, come here quick."

Gracie's request and another loud moan caused Sammy to jump up and head into Flodell's room.

A jovial atmosphere had filled the room, but when Sammy peeked in the door with a somber look on his face, it changed. "I don't think Flodell is going to make it."

"Oh, no!" Watema exclaimed.

The bright feeling faded to a dark black mood.

Caleb walked into the front room as fast as his artificial legs would allow. Most of the family members followed him. They looked on helplessly as Flodell stopped breathing for long periods and went limp, then when all hope was gone, she started back to breathing. Sammy stood at the foot of the bed trying to bring the baby into the world.

"Brother Solomon, Watema, Jonathan, and Maria, y'all go to the backroom and start praying," Sammy said, looking up. "The only way Flodell will pull through is by grace from the Lord. Gracie and Louisa can help in here."

Quickly, the four who were going to pray, left the room.

*   *   *

After Flodell's long struggle, Samuel helped a tiny infant enter the world. "A boy," he announced. "Gracie take this baby into the kitchen and clean him up"

Gently, Gracie took the baby and rushed to the kitchen. She looked out the window and remarked, "Baby, you came into the world with a snowstorm."

"*Oktusha,* (snow)," Caleb muttered.

Sammy called, "We're going to need both of those shirts. There's gonna be twins. Put a string around his wrist so we'll know he came first. Then wrap him in one of those shirts."

"Oh, no!" Caleb exclaimed, clamping his hand on his forehead.

"We'll help," Louisa said. "You've got plenty of kinfolks who'll lend a hand."

"If this other baby is born before we lose Flodell, it's for the best." Sammy stood over Flodell and spoke loudly to her. "Flodell, you have a baby boy. Do you hear me?"

Flodell lifted her head an inch or so.

"Help me get the other one into the world. You're having twins."

Flodell opened her eyes and pushed weakly. "O-o-o-h," she moaned, and then she collapsed.

"I don't think she'll make it," Sammy confided to Caleb. "Lean over her and talk to her. Try to keep her awake."

"Okay." He bowed over Flodell's face. "Wake up so you can see our new baby." He called to Gracie. "Gracie, bring the baby in here."

Gracie brought the baby in wrapped in Caleb's shirt. She held him to Flodell's face. "See, this is your baby boy. And there's another one on the way. Touch baby Snow's fingers." Gracie put the baby close to Flodell's face so she could feel his skin against hers.

"What-is-it?" Flodell asked, weakly.

"A boy," Gracie answered. "He looks like you."

"And here's his brother," announced Sammy. "Flodell, you're got two boys. Open you eyes and look this way. See?" He held the second baby up. "Louisa, take him in and clean him up. Be sure you wrap him in the other shirt. I'll take care of Flodell."

Louisa took the infant from Sammy and rushed with him to the kitchen.

"Look outside and see if it's still snowing," Caleb said.

Gracie opened the door and a gust of wind blew in. "It's still snowing, but the wind is up."

"*Mahli* (wind)," Caleb said.

By now the older baby was bawling loudly. Caleb stood over Flodell, washing her face with a wet rag. She was unresponsive. Her eyes rolled back and her head fell to the side. She collapsed again.

"We're about to lose her," Sammy whispered. "Talk to her. Tell her about the babies."

"Mama, you've got two babies," Caleb said. "Two handsome papooses. God gave you two babies to raise. Wake up so you can see them." He bent closer to her face. "I love you. I need you to help take care the babies."

Gracie and Louisa brought the newborns to Flodell. Gracie put one in the crook of Flodell's left arm. Louisa laid the other brother beside him.

"Look," Caleb said. He held up the arm of the first baby. "See this string? It's on *Oktusha*. We need to keep the string on his wrist."

Flodell's eyelids fluttered for a second. Then she closed them. "What-do-they-look-like?" she whispered.

"Like Indian braves," Caleb answered. "They both have lots of black hair. And they're skin is red and wrinkled, but they're handsome." After a while, he took the babies from Flodell's arm and walked into the room where the other four were praying. Sammy heard him clear his throat and say softly, "Look up here a minute. See the twins."

"Oh, how sweet," Watema said.

"Why don't y'all come in here to pray for Flodell? She's unconscious," Sammy called to Watema and the others. "Come on in. Lay your hands on her. Someone hold her hand, somebody touch her forehead, and so on, while Brother Solomon prays."

Brother Solomon dropped to his knees and took Flodell by the hand. He interceded for her health and well being. He thanked God for the live twins. His prayer ended with a request that the Lord's will be done.

"A-men," chorused several voices.

"She's in the Hands of the Lord," Sammy said.

He turned to Louisa and Gracie. "Your next job is to find milk for the babies. Caleb, who's the closest neighbor with a fresh cow? Send Maria and Jonathan to get milk. The babies need to get milk, even if the weather is bad."

When the couple returned and before Maria had dusted the snow from her clothes, she handed over the jar of milk. Quickly, Gracie warmed the milk and poured a small amount into a cup. Maria stood watching as Gracie and Louisa each dipped a clean soft cloth in the milk and dribbled the warm liquid in the babies' mouths. When the newborns seemed full, the two women dressed them in gowns. Louisa snuggled one infant on a pillow placed inside a drawer taken from the bureau. She pulled out another drawer for the second baby. The drawers rested on chairs in the kitchen, to keep the babies warm.

Maria felt tired, but determined to see the drama end well. Into the night, she watched Sammy continuing to work with Flodell. Caleb massaged her arms and hands.

In the wee hours of the morning, Flodell started tossing around.

She reached her right hand out, feeling of the mattress. "The baby?" she asked.

"Asleep," Caleb answered. "Do you want to see them?"

"Them?" Flodell asked.

"Yes. Twin boys. I'm calling them *Oktusha* and *Mahli*, until you name them," Caleb answered.

Sammy smiled at Caleb. "Bring *Oktusha* and *Mahli* in. She'll do better when she sees them."

"Praise the Lord," Caleb exclaimed.

Double Praise the Lord.

Chapter Twenty-Five

$\mathcal{M}$aria woke up late the day after Christmas to find Sammy and Louisa still asleep. The wild ride everyone had taken only hours earlier had taken its toll. Later, while the Grant family ate breakfast, Brother Solomon and Watema arrived. They stayed over for another day to learn how Flodell fared and because of the snow covering the roads. Jonathan's request to marry Sammy's daughter must wait.

Concerned about her upcoming marriage, Maria frowned when she watched Sammy leave. He said he must go to Doc Coleman's to ask him to visit Flodell. The new mother's health was more important *at this moment,* than Jonathan asking for her hand in marriage.

Sammy returned to tell the family that Doc believed Flodell would survive and be able to care for her babies. Since two babies and an ailing mama might be a handful for Granny Wade, Gracie volunteered to help care for them. She asked Sammy to drive her home to get a few necessities. Would there ever be a spare moment for Jonathan to speak with Papa?

What if they get stuck? Maybe Papa is suspicious about Jonathan and me.

After Sammy and Gracie returned, the excitement settled down. Jonathan came to Maria's to ask Sammy for permission to marry his daughter. Maria held her breath when she saw Sammy frown. "She's too young to get married," Sammy said. Maria's heart almost stopped beating.

Oh, no. Please, Dear God. Do I have to run away again?

"But—," Sammy said. He stood and offered his hand to Jonathan. "You are a good choice, so I'm giving my permission. Congratulations."

Thank You, Dear God.

The couple, elated with Sammy's consent, found a solitary place to celebrate. They spent a while making plans for their lives together after their wedding day. They agreed the ceremony would take place January 16th.

"I don't know if I can preach tomorrow," Jonathan confided to Maria. "I'm too much in love."

"So preach a sermon on love," Maria suggested.

"I don't have time to prepare a new sermon," Jonathan protested.

"With all the love going on around here, just give some personal testimonies," Maria said.

"I'll pray about it," Jonathan said. "Let's go to the church so I can practice."

Using Brother Solomon's car, they went to the church and slipped inside. Jonathan took Maria in his arms and kissed her.

Maria pulled away from his embrace long enough to ask, "Is this how you practice for a sermon?"

Jonathan laughed. "That's just the introduction to the sermon," he said. "Seriously, I'm praying about preaching a message based on Romans 8:28. What do you think of that?"

"It sounds perfect for people like Gracie. I'm sure everybody will be interested, because I've heard lots of Christians quote the first part of the verse. That was the most important part to me, before Papa explained the whole verse to Gracie and me."

"I don't know if I can explain it or not," Jonathan admitted, "but whatever the Lord wills, that's what I want to preach."

After they left the church, Maria and Jonathan stopped at Caleb's for a short visit. Silently, Maria thanked the Good Lord that Flodell seemed better. Flodell couldn't lift the babies but she gazed lovingly at them when Caleb brought them in for Maria and Jonathan to see.

"I don't think Flodell's well enough yet to decide what to name the boys," Caleb said. "There's no big hurry. We'll call them *Oktusha* and *Mahli* till she can pick out names."

"They're gonna be *Oktusha and Mahli*," Flodell said, weakly. "I'll decide on the rest of their names later."

"Whatever you say," Caleb said, and smiled. "They're handsome, ain't they?"

"Very handsome," Maria said. "Let me hold *Oktusha*."

Carefully, Caleb placed the older baby in Maria's arms. A flutter of love stirred her heart. The babies weren't her blood brothers, but she loved them all the same. If she and Jonathan lived in Riverview after they married, she could help Flodell care for them. After all, Caleb was her papa. She touched the red string tied around the baby's wrist. "That should never be taken off," she warned.

"Yeah. Your pa went through lots of torture because he didn't know if he was the oldest twin or not," Caleb said. "Course, these boys ain't been offered to the Lord to be preachers, I don't guess.

"Just thinking about yesterday and last night, you might say I was at the jumping-off place," Caleb confessed. "I knew that with these artificial legs, I couldn't chase two boys around, but God answered prayer. He brought Flodell back to life. Now she can do the running." He looked at Flodell and smiled. "Can't you?"

Flodell gave a faint nod.

"Most Christians come to places where it seems like they can't go on," Jonathan said. "I read somewhere that if you're on the edge of a cliff, 'God will catch you when you fall or He'll teach you to fly.' When I first met Maria, she had just been pulled back from her jumping-off place."

"Yeah, I felt like I stood on the edge of the world, ready to jump out into the dark," Maria agreed.

"But Mama and Papa had a real jumping-off place when Papa almost drove the car off in the creek the first time they went to Sandy Hill."

"I had one the night Luther froze to death," Gracie added, softly.

Maria tucked the blanket under *Oktusha's* chin. He felt warm and cuddly. How did all this happen to her?

"I ended up with a new papa. It's hard to believe you're my real papa," she said. She looked at Caleb and blinked back tears. "Two papas! Two baby brothers. I'm really blessed. That's not all. Soon I'll have a new husband. What do you think of Jonathan and me getting married?"

"With two new babies in the house, I don't know if I'm old enough to have a married daughter, but I sure do like Jonathan."

"We're getting married January 16th." She glanced over at Gracie, who was pulling out colorful pieces of cloth from a ragbag. "Gracie, you sure are quiet. Taking care of these babies got you worn out?"

"Well, it keeps me busy," Gracie admitted. What are you doing?"

"When Sammy took me home to get a few things, I brought my quilt scraps along. I'm picking out pieces of material big enough for quilt blocks," Gracie answered. "While the babies are sleeping, I keep busy cutting out blocks, but Teency and Tuffy are jealous. They want me to pay attention to them." She picked up Teency and rubbed her coat. Then she held the dog out to Jonathan.

"Here, you take Teency for a minute. I want to show Maria some scraps of cloth." Holding up a long piece of flowered cloth, she said, "Just look at this piece of cloth. Would you believe this could be made into something useful?"

"A quilt block?" Maria asked.

"Two or three quilt blocks. I can cut out several and sew them together. I can make a pattern like you see in a log cabin quilt or a flower pattern. I like flower designs the best."

Maria began to see the picture. Take a dozen or more pieces and put them together into a design. Then keep repeating the design and sew them together. They made up a quilt top.

"Why, Gracie, that's another example of all things working for good!" Maria exclaimed.

"You are exactly right," Jonathan said. "Even though the piece is going into a quilt, it illustrates that all things can work together for good."

"Because all the pieces put together will make a beautiful quilt," Maria said. She turned to Jonathan. "Be sure and remember that for your sermon," she said, petting Teency.

He nodded in agreement.

"Sure glad my scraps will help teach a lesson, as well as keep someone warm," Gracie said.

Maria returned the baby to Caleb. Jonathan set Teency on the floor. They said good-bye to everyone and returned to Sammy's for supper. Jonathan didn't stay as long as Maria would have liked, but she knew he must prepare for tomorrow's sermon. After he left, Maria told Sammy that the lamp he'd used the night before was a Christmas gift from her and Louisa. He had already set it on a table near his chair.

*   *   *

The morning of January 16th turned out to be beautiful. Members of the Grant family, the Wade family, Brother Solomon, Watema, and Austin assembled to view the wedding of Jonathan Folsom and Maria Grant. Jenny and Bailey Wesley came. They had fallen in love at Brother Solomon and Watema's wedding. Caleb and Flodell, along with Gracie, slipped in at the last minute. Smiles covered the new parents' faces as they glowed with happiness. Gracie helped out by carrying one of the babies.

Grandpa Tobias Grant had been asked to perform the ceremony. Sammy's twin brother, Toby, played the organ while Maria walked down the aisle. She wore the beautiful purple wedding dress belonging to Flodell. Jonathan looked the part of a groom, dressed in his preacher suit. Maria's aunt, Hallie Maytubby, had brought a locket, the family heirloom carried over the Trail of Tears, for Maria to wear during the ceremony. Maria felt as if she were floating in a dream world. Everything was perfect!

After the wedding, Gracie came to speak with Jonathan and Maria. "I'm enrolling in nursing school."

"You don't mean it!" Maria exclaimed.

"Yes, while I've been helping take care of Flodell and the babies, I realized I could still be useful, even without a husband." Gracie fought back the tears. "So, I'm leaving to go to school.

"Y'all can live in my house if you want to. Just take care of White Lightning and the two dogs. And in the spring, take care of the flowers. Because I learned that '. . . all things work together for good to them that love God, to them who are the called according to *his* purpose.' For everyone of us, even me.

"You want to live in my house?"

Maria gazed into Jonathan's eyes. "Do we?"

"I can't answer that right now, but we can stay there while we're deciding about our future.

"Can't we, Mrs. Folsom?" Jonathan asked, giving his new bride a tight squeeze.

"We sure can, Mr. Folsom," Maria answered.